RAFE PRESSED HER BODY AGAINST HIS OWN . . .

"Soon," she whispered, "soon I will be yours." And separating herself from him, she took his right hand. "Come with me," she said.

With incredible swiftness, Inanna led him to a grotto deep in the mountains. There she opened her naked thighs for him, making him forget all the other women he had ever known, and receiving from him a pleasure so intense that her body quivered with ecstasy. . . .

Here where god and man melted into one . . .

The Gods' Temptress

A soaring novel of destiny
and desire

P9-DTM-232

The Gods' Temptress

by Irving A. Greenfield

A Dell Book

Published by
Dell Publishing Co., Inc.
1 Dag Hammarskjold Plaza
New York, New York 10017

Dell ® TM 681510, Dell Publishing Co., Inc.

ISBN: O-440-14275-X

Printed in the United States of America

First printing—October 1978

The Gods' Temptress

I

Rafe never knew his father or mother, or if he was an only child, or if he had brothers and sisters elsewhere. Sometime during his very early years he was taken by Gumpa in a raid and brought to the stronghold, to live among Gumpa's people. Rafe had no memory of the event, though it was the second most momentous incident in his life; the first, of course, was his birth of which the gods mercifully denied him memory.

He was some years older before he learned that Gumpa seldom took captives of any age. But when he did, they were always sacrificed to the gods of his people. The reason Rafe survived, he was later told by Pagar, Gumpa's oldest son, was that the flames drew away from him when it came his turn to die in the fire.

Gumpa was so impressed with what he and the other men saw that despite the vehement objections of Borit, the priest, he dashed into the fire and brought the child out.

Later, to honor the memory of his friend, who had died fighting at his side, Gumpa named the boy Rafe. And thus Rafe lived with Gumpa's people, eventually learning that he did not belong to them.

Rafe was sheltered by Gumpa and ate at his table. When Gumpa taught his sons to ride and hunt, he also taught Rafe. Gumpa was quick to recognize that Rafe would soon be as good as he—and he was by far the best in the stronghold.

He praised Rafe's skill and took such pride in having him as part of his family that he was seriously thinking of having him become a son by adoption.

This ceremony would have taken place the following spring, when the sun would stand midway between the end of winter and the beginning of summer. Then, by Rafe's own reckoning, he would have been no less than seventeen and not more than twenty years old.

Rafe looked forward to becoming Gumpa's son. But it never happened and one winter's day the course of his life was forever changed. . . .

The sun that morning was very bright and halfway up the sky, when the men led their horses out of the stronghold. The women and children followed, but only for a short distance. Then they stopped and watched the line of grim-faced men form a circle around Gumpa, their chieftain.

Borit, the priest, also watched. He stood on the walkway behind the palisade. Several times he closed his eyes. In a strange tongue, he mumbled prayers of thanksgiving to Urd, the dread God of Darkness. Then with a smile on his thin lips, he whispered, "The spell is tightly wound and will run its course. . . . This time I will triumph . . . this time I will gain more than I had before . . . this time, Rafe, I will destroy you!"

The breath of the men and their horses steamed in the cold air. Now and then a horse snorted or pawed restlessly at the ground. The animals sensed something important was about to happen. They were filled with the same kind of tenseness that came to them before they went galloping into a fight.

The men too were tense, waiting for Gumpa to

judge whether their horse would live or die. But they knew that such a judgment was necessary, if some of them were to survive the winter.

That year it had turned cold almost at the end of summer. After several severe nights, most of what the women had grown froze before it could be harvested. Everywhere the trees had given up their leaves early. By the time winter had truly come, food was very scarce. It was so cold that the river, which lay on one side of the stronghold, was covered over with ice so thick it could bear the weight of many riders and their horses.

Gumpa lost no time. He began to judge as soon as the circle was formed around him. A nod indicated the horse would live, and a slight shake of his head that it would die. Often he reached out and stroked the animal's face, even though he had chosen death for it. And sometimes he said a few words to the owner, hoping to comfort him, since all his people were strongly bound to their horses.

Rafe stood close to his chestnut stallion, Agni. He did not have to whisper into his ear to quiet him, nor did he have to put his hand on him. A look from Rafe was enough for him to know what he was expected to do and he would do it.

Gumpa was the only other man in the stronghold who could control his horse as easily. Many of the people said Rafe was more like Gumpa than any of his own sons, though there was no physical resemblance between them. Rafe was taller than Gumpa. His eyes and hair were black, while Gumpa's eyes and hair were brown. But Rafe had his easy gait and he rode like him, making his body and that of the horse into a single entity.

Suddenly Rafe found Gumpa standing in front of him. His eyes peered into Rafe's. Neither man spoke.

But as Rafe waited for the decision, he watched the look on Gumpa's face change from that of a man determined to do what must be done to an expression of bewilderment; as if he saw something he could not understand. Gumpa quickly recovered himself and, moving his eyes from Rafe to Agni, he signaled with a nod that the animal should be spared.

Rafe never asked Gumpa what he saw, but the chieftain was so disturbed by it that toward twilight, he sought out Borit, the priest.

Borit had come to the stronghold some weeks before Rafe's capture. Like so many other men who gave their lives to the gods, he had said nothing about his past, or where he had been previously. But from his sun-darkened skin, Gumpa knew the priest had recently been south, where the sun gave a man's skin that color, or turned it a blistery red.

Borit had arrived at the stronghold shortly after Eris, the previous priest, had suddenly sickened and then died. Gumpa had allowed Borit to stay for a trial period, during which he had to prove his powers. In a matter of weeks, he had shown himself to be more powerful than the old priest. He could summon up a storm, bring a terrible wind, and see into the future. . . .

Borit lived alone in a small house on the edge of the river at the far end of the stronghold. He was a thin man of moderate height. His eyes were cloud-gray and his hair was white.

He welcomed Gumpa as if he were expecting him and in a low but distinct voice, he said, "I still have some mead left and would be honored to share it with you."

Gumpa graciously declined the offer and moved to the hearth to warm his hands.

"I was told you judged well this morning," Borit said.

"As well as any man could," Gumpa answered, facing the priest. "I hope those I chose to live will in the spring be proof of my wisdom."

"Only the gods are wise," Borit said. "A man can only hope to be fortunate." His voice was cold.

Gumpa nodded. Lately, he had begun to feel uncomfortable in the company of the priest, without knowing why.

"You look troubled," Borit commented.

"These are woeful times," Gumpa replied with a deep sigh. "I cannot ever remember the river freezing over with such thick ice."

"Nor can I," Borit said. "I have asked Freyer—"

"Yes . . . yes, I know you have," Gumpa told him. "I did not come here to ask you to do any more than you have." He hesitated for several moments before he said, "I need your skill to help me understand what I have seen."

Borit gestured toward the table.

Gumpa sat down and set his elbows on the top of the table.

Borit sat across from him. He was a patient man. He had waited almost twenty years for this visit. And now that it was taking place, he savored every moment of it. His revenge was almost within his grasp.

"This morning," Gumpa said, "at the judging I saw in the eyes of one of the men something that happened a long time ago, only . . . though the event was the same, the people in it were reversed." He looked questioningly at the priest.

Borit rubbed his scanty beard. A flicker of light darted into his gray eyes. "I must know the event and the people in it," he told him.

"Rafe," Gumpa said, "before I named him. When he was placed in the fire and the flames drew back . . . But this time, the flames did not draw back and I was consumed by them."

11

"And Rafe did nothing?"

"Nothing."

Borit closed his eyes and slowly began to sway from side to side. "The gods are angry," he intoned. "They are very angry."

Gumpa remained silent. He had seen the priest go into a trance many times. But it had never happened so quickly. . . . Borit's swaying made him uneasy. He tried to move his eyes to the far wall, where the priest had hung his shield and battle-ax, but found he could not. Borit's movements transfixed him. The room was suddenly much smaller and the warmth from the hearth disappeared.

"Once you denied the gods what was rightfully theirs," Borit said. "Now they are angry."

"But why now, after so many years?" Gumpa asked.

"It is their anger," Borit answered.

"And what will end their anger?"

Borit's swaying became more violent. Then suddenly he leaped to his feet and, flinging his arms up, as if he were fending off a blow, he cried out, "You ask too much . . . too much!"

Gumpa sucked in his breath.

Twisting and turning, Borit staggered around the room. He foamed at the mouth, shouted strange words, and rolled his eyes. And then he cried out, "Ask something else. . . . No . . . No . . . He was soon to become his son." Then he dropped to the floor, balled his body as a child might, and shuddered. He moaned as if some unseen presence was flogging him.

Slowly Gumpa got to his feet. He was wet with sweat and chilled to the bone at the same time. He took several deep breaths. The room regained its former size and he again felt the warmth from the hearth on his back. Shaken by Borit's words, he went to the priest and gently laid his hand on the shoulder of the trembling man.

"It is Gumpa," he said softly. "Gumpa, the chief of the stronghold . . . Come, Borit . . . You have served me well."

After a while, the priest stopped trembling and, opening his eyes, he looked up at Gumpa. "The gods want—"

"Yes," Gumpa spoke softly. "I know what the gods want."

"And will you give him to them?"

With a slow nod, Gumpa said, "If he is caught, I will give him to them. . . . But I will not deliver Rafe to the flames as if he were a stranger."

Borit sat up.

Gumpa helped him to his feet and led him to the table.

"The gods ask most from those they love most," Borit said.

Gumpa did not answer, though had he, he would have told the priest that the gods always took for themselves the best men, the best women, and the best horses, and gave very little in return for what they took. . . .

The stronghold became a sad place indeed. No day passed without Death pausing to take one of the very young, the very old, or the very sick.

Sometimes in the twilight when Rafe stood on the high ground to the north of the stronghold, he could see Death lead those for whom he came away from the camp. They followed behind him as he did a small dance.

Once Rafe was sure he heard the scrannel sound of his pipe and it brought prickles to his back.

Another time the last one in Death's troupe turned to him. It was Tarki, a man Rafe's own age, who had come down with a fever two days before and now was dead. He raised his arms toward him, as if Rafe could reach across the distance between life and death and somehow pull him back.

Rafe almost did reach out for him, but the next instant the twilight deepened and Death and those who followed Death that day vanished.

Rafe never mentioned to anyone that he had seen Death. He did not want to cause any more grief to the people who had sheltered and fed him than the gods had already set on them. But he sensed that Borit knew he had seen Death.

In the days that had passed since the fullness of summer, Rafe had watched Gumpa change from a tall man with an open face and laughter in his deep brown eyes, to someone with bent shoulders and a strange, haunted look in his eyes.

Then one night, when Rafe was seated with Gumpa and his sons at the big table, he sensed a certain uneasiness. From time to time, Gumpa glanced at him but did not speak. And his sons, who were usually boisterous, spoke to each other in muted tones. The crackling of the fire was louder than their voices while, outside the hall, the wail of the wind sounded like a death chant.

Rafe did not break the silence.

Gumpa sighed deeply. Several times he moved his hand across his grizzled beard. Though the reddish glow from the fire flowed over his face, it was still full of shadows.

Whatever Gumpa wanted to say to Rafe, he could not find either the words or the courage to say, though in the past he had always possessed an abundance of both. One by one his sons stood up and drifted to their pallets.

After a while, Gumpa and Rafe silently faced each other across the table.

Gumpa looked up and shook his head. As his eyes came to rest on Rafe again, he still did not speak. Then he stood up and went to where he slept in the hall.

The fire burned low and the night was suddenly colder. Rafe walked to his pallet. He lay down on his bed of animal skins, drawing the heaviest one over him to shield himself from the chill.

The children slept closest to the hearth. Everyone else's place had been chosen by Gumpa. Astrid, the young woman who would soon become his wife, slept with the other women. Since Rafe was not blood-related to Gumpa, his place was against the far wall of the shelter, directly opposite the heavy oaken door.

Rafe could not sleep. His stomach growled with hunger. In the semidarkness, he stared up at the cross-beams and wondered what Gumpa had wanted to say.

After a while Rafe's eyes closed and in a dream he saw Gumpa mount Astrid. A sudden heat flashed in his groin and his heart beat faster.

Before Gumpa bought Astrid from her parents, Rafe would often watch her swim naked in the river. Once he had even tried to catch her, but she had managed to run back into the camp before he could.

Rafe had already had many women under him, but none had ever meant enough to him to make her his wife. Besides, he could not have a wife until he either captured one in a raid, or he became Gumpa's son and bought one.

He heard Astrid moan and Gumpa grunt with plea-sure. Suddenly Rafe was awake. He listened for their sounds. But all was silence again, except for the sound of everyone breathing which was punctuated now and then by Gumpa's loud snoring.

II

Asleep once more, Rafe let his spirit call Gumpa's and it quickly came. Once more they sat across from one another at the table. The fire in the hearth was only red embers. Everyone else in the great hall was wrapped in their own dreams. This time he knew what Gumpa wanted to say without his having to say it. The words were in his eyes; they mingled with his unshed tears, "Soon you will have to leave the camp, Rafe; I cannot keep you with me much longer."

Gumpa meant no harm. What food there was had to be given to his sons and daughters and their children. They must survive if his line was to continue.

Rafe nodded, hoping Gumpa's spirit would see the nod and understand it. Then to be sure, he whispered, "A few days more and I will be gone."

The vision faded. Rafe turned on his side and, closing his eyes, he quickly drifted into a contented sleep.

The next morning Gumpa sat down next to Rafe and said, "I dreamed we spoke last night."

"Yes," Rafe answered, "we did."

"Did I say anything to injure you?" he asked.

Rafe shook his head and told him, "There were tears in your eyes."

"And sadness in my heart," he said, touching his chest.

"Then no more must be said," Rafe replied.

"Are you afraid?"

Rafe was not, though he knew he should have been.

When game had been plentiful, it had been difficult, though not impossible, for a man to survive away from his people. But at a time like this when game was scarce, he might not have a chance. He could expect to be treated as an enemy by all people, even those who had once been his own. And should he be captured, he could expect either to be sacrificed to the gods or eaten. Perhaps both.

Suddenly it occurred to Rafe that could be what Gumpa hoped would happen. . . . Once he left the camp, the men in it would be free to hunt him down as if he were a stranger.

Gumpa realized what Rafe was thinking and he said, "I will hold them from you as long as possible."

Rafe did not know what to say and remained mute.

"Other than Borit, you are the only one among us not of our blood," Gumpa said. "The gods will not have their priest or one of us."

Rafe nodded. He knew their laws. He had taken part in several hunts where the quarry had been a man. None had ever gotten away. Though he had hunted them, he had never reveled in their deaths as had Gumpa and his people. Listening to a man scream as fire chewed at his body had not made him feel the presence of the gods. And though he had never questioned their blood rites, he had always felt alien to them.

"You are skilled enough not to be taken," Gumpa said.

"And what if I should have to kill one of them?" Rafe asked.

"It is understood that you will do everything to prevent them from taking you."

"Will you lead the hunt?"

17

Gumpa shook his head and told him, "Pagar will lead the men who will come after you."

Rafe uttered a deep sigh.

And Gumpa made an open gesture with his hands to signify he had nothing more to say.

Rafe turned and started back to his pallet for his weapons. From now on, they would have to be his constant companions.

He knew what he would be expected to do. . . . On a particular day in the near future, he would leave the stronghold and if he did not return by twilight, the hunt for him would begin the following morning. . . .

Later that day Rafe returned to the hall. Except for Astrid, it was empty. When he passed her, she called him by name.

Rafe stopped and turned to her.

Boldly Astrid threw back the skin bedcover and revealed her nakedness. Her breasts were round and high. There was a hint of a smile on her full lips.

"He is an old man, Rafe," she whispered. "If you kill Gumpa, you will be the chieftain and you will have me." She spread her naked thighs to show him the place where she would give him pleasure.

Rafe knelt down and moved his right hand over her firm warm breasts, down her stomach, and then over the opening of her sex. It was already wet.

She snapped her thighs shut, trapping his hand between them. "No one will stand against you," she said in a breathy voice. "No one."

Rafe shook his head. Had he become Gumpa's son, she in turn would have become his mother. . . . He pulled his hand out from between her warm thighs.

She laughed softly.

Rafe took his weapons and ran from the hall.

18

III

The rest of that day, the next, and the one that followed were sunless, bitter cold, and full of wind. Rafe hunted, hoping to make a kill that might stay his departure a while longer. But he failed to find a single trail. The other hunters were no more successful than he. The people in the camp ate roots and the bark of trees.

And at twilight, no matter on what side of the camp Rafe stood, he saw Death. Each evening the line that followed him was longer than the previous one.

Those days and nights were also a time of great restlessness for him. He did not want to think about what Astrid had said. But her words were always with him, especially at night when in the darkness of the shelter he would dream of Gumpa mounting her and listen for his low growl of pleasure.

Rafe had never wanted to be anything more than Gumpa's son. But now, spurred by Astrid's offer, he began to see the possibility of a different future for himself.

Rafe knew that Gumpa's father's father became chieftain by killing his predecessor. It was not uncommon then, or even now, for a man to become the leader of a people that way. Usually it was a stranger who came and offered the challenge. In all Rafe's years with Gumpa's people he had only seen one man challenge Gumpa.

He had just passed his twelfth year. The man came to the stronghold. He was big and wild-looking. Some of the people said he had lived among the huge rocks at the edge of the forest.

He had challenged Gumpa and the two of them had fought in a flat open space surrounded by all of the people in the camp.

Each of them had taken wounds. The air rang with the sound of the swords crashing, one against the other. Twice, the blades had shattered from the mighty blows.

The ground beneath their feet had become stained with blood. Gumpa had not only fought for his life, but also for the lives of his sons. If he had lost, they too would have been killed.

Both men had become tired and the stranger, realizing he could not best Gumpa, had turned and fled.

Gumpa had gone after him and driven his sword into the stranger's back. The man had still been alive when he was sacrificed to the gods. . . .

Rafe realized that if he did kill Gumpa, he would also have to kill Pagar and the rest of his brothers, or suffer death at their hands. Perhaps torture before being sacrificed. From moment to moment his resolve to raise his sword against Gumpa vacillated depending on how afraid he felt of dying in the attempt to become a chieftain.

Rafe made several attempts to summon Astrid's spirit to him. All of them failed and whenever he saw her, she seemed to be totally unaware of his presence. He wanted her at least to look at him.

His feelings for Astrid did not blind him to the place he held at Gumpa's table. None of Gumpa's sons spoke to him. They no longer considered him there. And as for Gumpa, he did not have to speak; his eyes asked when Rafe would be leaving.

On the third night, Rafe did not join the others at

the table. Sitting near his pallet, he ate alone, munching on dried bark. When he was half asleep, he felt a warm breath against his cheek.

To prevent him from crying out, a small delicate hand came over his mouth.

"You must kill him soon," Astrid whispered. She took hold of his hand and placed it on her breast.

Rafe opened his eyes. She was gone! He bolted up. His eyes went to where Gumpa and his sons sat; then he looked at the smaller table where the women ate. Astrid was there.

Rafe lay down again. He did not understand what had happened. He had not summoned Astrid's spirit and yet it had come to him in a way so real that he had felt her breath against his face and held the softness of her breast in his hand.

He did not know if it was a good or a bad omen for Astrid to have sent her spirit to him. Had her spirit met his when he had summoned it, he would have been content to do nothing more than look at it. He would not have spoken to it about killing as hers had.

Suddenly Astrid left the table with two of the other women. She did not even cast her eyes in his direction.

Rafe started up. He was going to draw her attention to himself. But before he could do or say anything, he realized she was already facing him.

She said something to the other women and turned away.

In that moment Rafe knew he had been tricked. Some evil spirit had come to him in Astrid's form, not once but twice.

Rafe began to tremble.

To hide his fear, he slipped down on his pallet of skins and covered himself. When he finally slept, his head was filled with bloody phantoms. . . .

IV

~~~~~~

Rafe awoke before night gave way to the grayness of dawn. All around him the various members of Gumpa's family were still asleep. He looked toward the fire. And there in the column of smoke that rose from the glowing embers, he saw her, the evil spirit that had tried to possess him in Astrid's form.

She was almost too hideous to look at, yet he could not take his eyes from her distorted face. The right eye was lower than the left. Her mouth was a lipless wound. Her teeth were filed to points and she continually swirled her tongue around her fangs.

She seemed to be looking toward Gumpa. Then slowly she began to dance and make beckoning gestures toward him. Her movements became more alluring.

Gumpa moved in his sleep.

The spirit said something. But her words were meant only for Gumpa.

He became more restless.

Suddenly a child cried out.

The spirit stopped moving and looked toward the child. With a wave of her clawlike hand, she silenced it. Then she started to dance again. But after a few moments she stopped and turned toward Rafe.

Their eyes locked. Never had he beheld such malice.

She hissed at him. He could hear the blood pounding in his ears. He trembled like a leaf shaken by a strong wind. Now he saw her in a different light. There were snakes in her hair. The nipples of her sagging breasts dripped pus and the place between her naked thighs crawled with maggots.

The longer Rafe looked at her, the larger she became. Fearful she would overwhelm him, he cowered back against the side of the shelter. He tried to cry out but the sound remained caught in his throat.

She left the column of smoke and came toward him.

Rafe groped frantically for his spear, lifted it, and hurled it at her with all his strength. It whirred through the air and passed through her, coming down with a thud.

Gumpa groaned!

The spirit shrieked with laughter and disappeared into the smoke.

She had won; he had just killed Gumpa.

Within moments everyone in the shelter was awake.

Astrid began to scream. Gumpa's other wives joined her. Pagar, Kinsi, and Forra, Gumpa's three oldest sons, ran to their father.

Pagar knelt down and as he pulled the spear from Gumpa's back, there was a rush of blood.

Rafe clutched the hilt of his sword. He waited for Pagar and his brothers to attack. He was determined to die fighting. His heart raced; his chest heaved for air.

Pagar looked at him. Except for the spear in his hand, he and his brothers were unarmed. To show Rafe he did not intend to fight, he dropped the spear.

Rafe removed his hand from the sword's hilt.

Pagar motioned to his brothers. Following an old ritual, each one scooped up a handful of ashes from the fire and smeared their faces and arms with it. Astrid and Gumpa's other women did the same.

Then Pagar said in a quiet voice, "I am now chieftain. What belonged to my father is now mine. His weapons are mine. His women are mine and his children are mine."

Neither his brothers nor any other man contradicted him.

"My father will be burned on the funeral pyre with all he needs to be happy in the world of the dead," Pagar said.

Rafe waited until the body was taken from the shelter and all of the people were gone, before he gathered his weapons together. By the time he mounted Agni and rode out of the stronghold, it had begun to snow.

He could not have chosen a better time to leave since everyone else was occupied with Gumpa's funeral.

When Rafe gained the top of a distant hill, he looked back at the stronghold. But the falling snow was so dense, he could see nothing. He turned and rode down the far slope. Without delay, he had to put as much distance as possible between himself and the stronghold. . . .

V

The snow and wind grew worse. Rafe's eyebrows and beard were covered with snow. He had no idea where he was, or in which direction he was going.

Rafe dismounted and slowly led his unwilling horse through the deep snows.

Now and then Agni pulled up his head and snorted protestingly. He was telling him it was foolish to be out in the storm, that only a man possessed by demons would be abroad on such a day.

Rafe answered his objection by roughly pulling down on the reins. He was in no mood to offer an explanation to him. He too was cold; he too was hungry; he too was weary of pushing his way through the snow and breasting the buffeting wind.

The ashen light deepened until it was dark gray, though by his reckoning it could not have been much later than midday. Despite his robes of skin, Rafe was pained by the intense cold, especially his fingers and toes. The snow on his beard became ice.

Agni stumbled.

Rafe stopped and looked at him. His dark mane was covered with snow. There were bits of ice around his nostrils. And he was trembling from the cold.

Using the tracks make by his own footsteps, Rafe walked back to him.

Agni snorted and, shaking his head, he looked at him ruefully.

Rafe rubbed his face and said, "We must go on. . . . I must put as much distance between myself and the stronghold as possible." A sudden gust of wind threw him off balance. To prevent himself from falling, he flung his arms around Agni's neck.

Agni snorted again.

"There is no shelter nearby," Rafe said, regaining his feet. "We must continue." And taking hold of the reins again, he retraced his steps. But Agni would not move, though Rafe tugged hard at the reins.

With a defiant neigh, Agni reared up, tore loose from Rafe's hold, and angrily flailed the air with his forefeet. He was not going to go forward.

"All right," Rafe said, hoping to trick him, "we will go back."

Agni snorted loudly and shook his head.

"Then come with me and we will find shelter," Rafe told him.

Agni neighed loudly; he was determined not to go anywhere.

Rafe shrugged and walked away from him. He glanced over his shoulder.

Agni was not following.

Rafe continued to walk. Then suddenly, when he looked back over his shoulder, he could no longer see Agni. There was a wall of falling snow between them.

He stopped and, squinting into the grayness, searched for the darker form of Agni. He saw nothing and the pelting snow bruised his face and eyes painfully.

Rafe began to sweat. Stupidly he had left his weapons on Agni's back. His sword was sheathed and tied to the saddle. A spear, bow, and quiver of arrows were fastened in their proper places.

All he carried on his person was a knife and though

it was as long as his hand was wide, it would be useless in anything but the closest kind of combat with a man. Unless he could hurl himself at some animal, he could not even use it for hunting.

The ice on Rafe's beard burned. He ran his fingers through it, but the ice quickly formed again.

He shouted Agni's name. But instead of his responsive neighing, all he could hear was the wail of the wind and the hiss of the falling snow.

Rafe looked at his footprints. They were almost obliterated by freshly fallen snow. Before they vanished altogether, he started back over them, muttering curses at Agni for his stubbornness. He swore he would flay him alive.

Rafe soon realized the trail he was following was much longer than any he could have left. He stopped and looked around him. There was someone else out in the storm.

He knelt down and looked closely at the footprints. They were not his; his would have been much larger and, even with the newly falling snow, much deeper.

Still kneeling, Rafe made another attempt to find Agni. The falling snow remained as impenetrable as ever.

He slowly stood up. The wail of the wind was all around him.

Rafe was certain that someone else was close by. But he was too frightened to call out. Until now he was sure that he had not been tracked by any of the men from the stronghold. But if it was not one of them, who else would have a reason to be out in the storm?

He sucked in his breath and listened more intently, hoping to hear the brittle crunch of a footfall in the snow, or some other sound that would betray whoever was there with him. He heard nothing more than the wail of the wind, the hiss of the snow, and the pounding of his own blood. He released the air from his lungs in a burst of icy whiteness, and, looking down at the footprints again, he saw they were as clear as they had been before.

Rafe wanted to run. But which way would he go? Where would he be safe from capture by Pagar and the other men?

There were no answers to those questions.

Out of desperation he shouted for Agni again and as if it were intent on destroying the sound of his voice, the shriek of the wind suddenly became louder than his call.

He looked down at the footprints.

They had not changed.

He was about to take his chances and run back in the direction from which he had come. But he had the strange sensation he was being told to follow the footprints.

"No," Rafe answered, shaking his head. "No, I want—" He stopped. Who was he answering?

Then in the hiss of the falling snow, a voice said, "Follow the footprints."

Rafe's hand went to his knife. Sweat poured from his body. "Who are you?" he shouted.

The scream of the wind became louder.

"Where are you?" he yelled.

"Follow the footprints," the hissing voice repeated from the depths of the falling snow.

Rafe glanced over his shoulder. The way behind him was a wall of white

"You tarry too long," the voice hissed.

He took several deep breaths and started to follow the footprints. As soon as he reached one set, the snow in front of him parted to reveal another, and still another. . . . Anxious to reach whoever he was tracking, Rafe quickened his pace. Soon he was running. The footprints continued. His feet felt a change in the terrain. Now he was going up a hill; down its far slope; then across a wide valley.

The bleak afternoon grayness thickened into night. And though the storm still raged, the footprints were always clearly set in front of him.

The snow began to lessen and then stopped falling altogether. The wind dropped and the heavy cloud cover became ragged, revealing huge open patches of star-filled sky.

When Rafe felt as if he could run no more, he saw Agni.

He was standing very still. Rafe slowed to a walk and, gulping huge draughts of air, he managed to call to him.

The horse remained motionless.

And then Rafe saw the old woman. Wrapped in a robe of skins, she was sitting close to Agni.

Suddenly Rafe realized the footprints he had been following ended where she sat. He stopped some distance from her and Agni. But even from where he was he could see Agni was dead—frozen—and that the crone was close to perishing from the cold.

Rafe circled them.

Agni was no more than stone now.

"Fool," Rafe muttered at him. "Fool, if you had followed me, you would still be alive." He touched the horse's face.

Agni had been given to him by Gumpa when he had been no more than a boy and the horse had been only a colt. Rafe had broken him. They had grown up together and had shared much. He moved his hand along the animal's flanks. He was filled with sorrow and hoped Agni's spirit would find rich pasture until his own spirit would come to claim him.

Rafe took his weapons from Agni's snow-covered back and gave his attention to the crone.

Death was standing some distance from her. With

his bony hand, he beckoned to her spirit.

Angered that he had already taken Agni's spirit, Rafe placed himself between Death and the hag.

He understood and, knowing that it was not yet time for him to claim Rafe's spirit, he disappeared into the night, leading Agni after him.

VI

Under the skin robe, the crone moved as if she were gathering the fire to her. And the flames bent toward her.

Rafe tried to catch a glimpse of her face.

But the way she had draped the covering over her head prevented him from seeing any of her features.

He fed the fire several large pieces of wood. The flames immediately attacked them.

Rafe looked toward the frozen body of Agni and then back toward the crone, wondering which of them had found the other?

In truth, Rafe would have much preferred to have Agni alive than the crone. Had Death spared him and taken her instead, he would have been able to resume his escape on horseback with the coming of the dawn. But as things now stood, he was the one who was saddled since he stood a good chance of having to carry the crone on his back.

That prospect made him shake his head. Impatiently he asked her who she was and where she came from.

She appeared not to have heard the questions.

Thinking she might be deaf, Rafe shoutingly repeated them. No sooner were the words out of his mouth, than they came swooping down at him from all directions, as if he and the crone were surrounded by mountains on all sides, when in fact they were on a plain.

As huge wings of sound beat the air above his head, he clapped his hands over his ears. But the din continued, growing louder and louder until it was thunder, until it was a hammer crashing down on his skull. He fell to the ground and, in a vain attempt to escape, tried to claw his way into the snow. But the snow had become hard.

Then suddenly all the sound was gone. Except for the crackling of the fire and his own whimpering, the night was silent. With his vision blurred by tears, he looked up at the crone.

She had not moved.

Rafe sat up. His ears were still ringing.

Then the crone said, "I have come a long way and still have a long way to go before I reach the end of my journey." Her voice came from the depths of the animal-skin covering.

Rafe heard it yet he was not sure she had spoken. It was as if a vagrant breeze had caused some dry leaves to rustle.

He nodded, but did not press her for any more information. From all that had befallen him, he was certain she was a witch woman, the kind that no real woman would ever befriend and that all men would fear.

Rafe tried to hide his fear and busied himself with the fire.

He intended to flee as soon as she was asleep. Perhaps if he were far enough away from her by the time she awoke, her spells would have no effect on him.

He realized that she had probably sent the spirit to dance in the smoke and make him hurl his spear, so that he would kill Gumpa. But Rafe could not even begin to guess what she wanted with him. He had no real claim to anything. He was no more than a hunter.

There were other men in the stronghold who possessed much more than he ever would.

But Rafe remembered once having been told by Borit that witch women sometimes cast a spell on a man for no other reason than to devour his man-thing. He had said a witch woman was very much like a spider that way.

Rafe decided that if she made any move to stop him, he would drive his sword into her. Though he might not be able to kill her, he hoped the wound might make her lose some of the power she held over him.

Despite his resolution to remain awake, his eyelids grew heavy and he struggled to keep them open. But sleep came and swept him along on its dark waters. Within moments Rafe was once again standing on the river bank looking at Astrid. . . .

She was naked. Her high breasts floated in the water. Her black hair glistened in the bright sunlight. She saw him and smiled.

His man-thing stirred and grew long. He beckoned to her.

"Swim with me," she called out.

"I will," Rafe answered and quickly stripped off his clothing. He entered the river. The water was warm and the current gentle. He moved toward Astrid. She did not swim away from him.

Their naked bodies touched.

She pressed herself against him. Caressing his man-thing with her hand, she told him to use her body as its sheath. "At least until it has been well used."

He scooped her up into his arms and carried her to a small patch of grass under a large oak tree. There he gently set her down.

For several moments Rafe did nothing but look at her. He touched her hard pink nipples with the tips of his fingers.

She sighed deeply and closed her eyes.

His hand glided down her flat stomach and, without pausing, continued until it closed over the river-wet mound of her womanhood.

Her body trembled and from her parted lips came a slight gasp of pleasure.

"Rafe," she whispered. "Rafe, I have dreamed of you so many, many times."

"And I of you," he responded, easing his fingers between her parted thighs. He found the lips of her womanhood and spread them.

Astrid raised her arms to him and, arching her body, she said, "Now!"

Rafe stretched out between her open thighs. Slowly he entered her body, delighting in its pulsating warmth and its marvelous liquidity. He wanted to go deeper into her.

She wrapped her bare legs around his back and made a soft sound of contentment.

He put his lips to one of her nipples.

"Ah Rafe," she moaned. "Rafe, I am soon to be Gumpa's wife."

Rafe tried to free himself from her embrace but his strength was no match for the deliciousness of her movements. The pleasure he was experiencing was too intense for him to cast aside.

She drew up her knees so that he might thrust deeper into her. She began to moan and thrash her head from side to side.

His body strained into hers. He could feel exquisite heat snake its way through his groin.

"Rafe . . . Rafe . . . Rafe."

"I am with you," Rafe answered. "Astrid, I am with you!" And clutching her fiercely to him, he released his fluid.

Before his eyes, Astrid began to dissolve. Rafe tried

to hold on to her but she vanished, leaving him on the bank of the river. . . .

Wet from his dream, he awoke with a start. For a moment or two, he did not know where he was. But as soon as he saw the crone, Rafe remembered.

The fire was very low. Rafe glanced toward the east. The gray of dawn would not come for a while. He looked at the crone. She seemed to be asleep. If he intended to flee, now was the time. He took up his weapons and made sure he would be able to draw his sword should he have to.

As quietly as possible, Rafe stood up. He was ready to steal silently away.

The crone cackled.

Rafe did not move.

She was awake.

His hand was already on the hilt of the sword.

"I am hungry," the crone said.

He did not answer.

"We will eat and then we will talk," she told him.

"There is nothing to eat," he told her.

She gestured toward Agni.

Rafe wondered whether he should take his chances and strike at her with his sword. Then suddenly the skin covering over her began to move. She was shaking her head. She knew what he was thinking and probably would be able to stop him from doing her any harm just by blinking an eye.

He set his weapons down and went to carve meat from Agni's flanks. Though he was able to cut into his body easily enough, no blood flowed. He carved off two generous pieces and returned to the crone.

In a short while, she was biting into chunks of horse-meat. The crone ate with the skin covering pulled low over her face. She devoured several pieces of meat with gusto and, licking her fingers, she said, "I have eaten my fill."

Though Rafe was hungry, he could not bring himself to eat.

She gestured toward the uneaten meat and said,
"His spirit will not hold it against you. . . . You did not
kill him to eat."

"I am no longer hungry," Rafe lied.

She cackled but did not insist that he eat. Instead,
she said, "My name is Talum and I am going on a
long journey, Rafe."

"How do you know my name?" he asked, starting
up.

She waved the question aside and bid him to sit
again.

"How do you know my name?" Rafe repeated.

"It is one of many names I know," she answered.
Astrid . . . Gumpa and even Pagar are three more."

"The dream—"

"A gift to you," she said, "for standing between me
and Death."

"I should have let him take you," Rafe growled.

Talum made no reply. Slowly she got to her feet.

"Where are you going?" Rafe asked.

"I must find some place to rest for a while," she
said.

Her cowl had slipped back and for the first time he
saw her face. It was as ugly as the face of the spirit
who had danced in the smoke. But it was very different. Her skin was nut brown and seamed with lines.
Her gums were toothless and on her chin there were
wisps of gray hair.

She held a staff in her right hand. It was painted
red, green, and yellow and it was incised with various
figures. The top of it was clearly carved into the
shape of a man-thing.

Rafe scrambled to his feet and said, "I cannot return to my stronghold."

"It is close by," she answered and pointed with the

top of the staff to the east, where dawn was already flooding the sky with a grayish light.

He was about to dispute her when he saw the stronghold. It was a short distance from where they were standing. The smoke from the various fires looked like the slender trunks of saplings.

All around them, the darkness was rapidly beginning to dissolve. And in the snow, he could see the remnants of his own footprints. They made circles within circles until they stopped where he had found Talum the previous night. He had never really moved far from the stronghold!

"The people are starving," he said, facing Talum. "They will not welcome us."

She started to walk.

Rafe fell in alongside of Talum. He tried to reason with her; he even told her that he would be killed if he went back. But Talum pretended not to hear him.

The snow was very deep and it was difficult to make their way through it. Several times she floundered in a drift and he pulled her free. By the time they reached the hill to the north of the stronghold, the sun was high in the morning sky. The glare from the snow forced him to squint in order to see.

Even before they entered the stronghold, he could hear the men shout, "It is Rafe. . . . Rafe has come back. . . . Rafe has come back . . . ." And then he saw Pagar and his brothers, Kinsi and Forra; they were running toward them with their swords drawn.

Rafe pushed Talum in back of him and, unsheathing his weapon, he stood his ground, ready to meet their attack.

Behind them were the other men and women of Gumpa's family. He did not see Astrid.

Pagar and his two brothers came to a halt in front of him, just beyond the reach of his sword.

VII

"We come only to rest," Rafe explained.

Pagar frowned, while his two brothers raised their eyebrows and glanced questioningly at each other. Their foreheads were still smeared with ashes.

"I will put up my sword and sheath it, if each of you will do the same," Rafe offered.

They did not reply.

"The old woman and I have been out in the storm. . . . Agni is dead, frozen and—"

"There is no one with you," Pagar said. "You are alone?"

Rafe quickly glanced over his right shoulder. Talum was not behind him. He was about to remonstrate and show them the two sets of footprints in the snow, when he realized that if she had vanished, her footprints would be gone too. He scanned the snow all the way to the gate of the stronghold. There were only his footprints. By taking hers with her, Talum had put him in the fell grasp of his enemies. . . . Rafe faced Pagar and his brothers.

"I would rather have taken you in a hunt," Pagar said.

Rafe nodded. There was a bond between them.

They were hunters. Pagar was, even in his looks, more like Gumpa than any of his brothers. Some in the stronghold had said of Forra, the youngest of the three, that he had not come from Gumpa's seed. He was fairer than the others. His hair was the color of straw.

"Put up your sword," Pagar said. "We will take you whether you fight or not."

"I will fight," Rafe answered without rancor. "The spirit of one or more of you will walk behind Death before the day is over."

His words made Kinsi, the middle brother, uneasy. He was a tall, thin man with amber eyes. He was not a good hunter. But his skill as a trader was unequaled by anyone else in the stronghold. He took several deep breaths before he said, "None here seek your blood. But the gods—"

"I will not go willingly to the gods," Rafe told him with a shake of his head.

"We are sorely pressed," Pagar said. "Though I stand in Gumpa's place, none can replace him."

"He was a strong and just leader," Rafe responded, honoring the man who would have been his father.

"His spirit has not gone with Death," Pagar said in a low, sad voice.

It was Rafe's turn to frown.

"What my brother told you is true," Kinsi said. "Gumpa's spirit will not go with Death."

"His spirit hovers above the ashes of the funeral pyre and calls your name," Pagar said. "He will speak to none of us."

Prickles flashed up Rafe's back. There were few things more terrible than the spirit of a dead man or woman that refused to follow Death. Such a spirit sought revenge and was always aided by the gods. Death, the supreme master of all humankind, was rendered powerless until the spirit was satisfied.

"He called to you," Forra said, "and when you are given to the gods he will have you and go his way."

"And Gumpa asks for nothing else?" Rafe questioned.

"Only you," Pagar answered.

"What does Borit, the priest, say of this?" Rafe asked.

"That you must be taken and sacrificed to the gods so that your spirit and Gumpa's will be together."

"Why would Gumpa want me?" Rafe asked. "I am not related to him by blood."

"Borit said the bond between you and Gumpa is stronger than blood," Kinsi said.

Rafe did not ask what bond could be stronger than blood; he already knew it was death. But he did not know what to say, much less what to do. Then suddenly it occurred to him that if Gumpa had accused him of his death, his sons would have met him with an anger so great that he would either have been dead by now, or on his way to be sacrificed. Gumpa wanted him for some reason other than his death. . . .

A crow made several circles over their heads and came down behind Rafe. It began to caw loudly. And in the raucous sounds of the bird's language, another voice was telling him to go and speak with Gumpa.

Pagar sensed something was happening and he asked Rafe why he suddenly looked so strange.

"I want to speak with Gumpa's spirit," Rafe said, giving more determination to the tone of his voice than he felt.

For a few moments Pagar hesitated but then he nodded.

"We will put up our swords," Rafe told him, "and not draw them until we must."

Pagar agreed and sheathed his weapon. His brothers followed suit.

VIII

Rafe led the way with Gumpa's sons close behind him and the people from the stronghold silently following them. The procession slowly wended past the burial ground to the hill where Gumpa's funeral pyre was still smoldering. Other than the crunching sound made by the many feet following him, all Rafe could hear was the drumlike pounding of his heart, which quickened with every step he took.

By the time he reached the base of the hill, the sun was gone and the sky had filled with dark clouds. A strong wind came howling down from the north. The swiftness of the change was a bad omen. But whatever it portended, Rafe had no choice but to face it.

"I and my brothers will go no farther," Pagar called out above the sound of the wind.

Rafe stopped and turned toward them.

"Gumpa calls for you," Kinsi shouted.

And Forra, gesturing toward the dark sky, yelled, "He wants you and only you."

Without answering, Rafe continued his climb to the top of the hill. The snow was very deep. He was wet with sweat and breathing hard long before he reached his goal.

Several times he had the feeling that he was far higher than the top of the hill. But he continued to climb. . . . Then suddenly, without any prior indication that he reached the top, he was there, looking down at the glowing embers of Gumpa's funeral pyre. He had expected to see Gumpa's spirit in some tangible form, either hovering over the ashes or close by, but he saw nothing.

He turned and looked toward the base of the hill. But the blowing snow prevented him from seeing anything.

It occurred to him that Pagar and his brothers might be trying to trick him. Alone on the hill, he could be taken easily. Men from the stronghold could come at him simultaneously from all sides. From such an attack as that, there would be no escape. . . . His hand went to his sword's hilt, when a sad voice called out, "Put by . . . Put by . . . You came in peace."

Wide-eyed and trembling with fear, Rafe faced the glowing ashes.

"You will not see me," Gumpa told him in a voice that seemed to come from under the shriek of the wind. "I am no longer of your world and not yet in Death's. . . . His patience grows short with me. . . . But Odin has stayed his taking of me a while longer." As the spirit spoke the red glow of the embers became darker and flames burst forth where there was nothing for them to burn.

Rafe dropped to his knees. "Forgive me, Gumpa," he pleaded, "my spear was not meant for you."

"It was," the voice moaned. "It was."

Rafe shook his head. "In the smoke of the fire," he explained, "I saw an evil spirit . . . I threw the spear at her."

"As she meant you to do," the voice said. "As it was foretold many, many years ago."

Beating his fists on the snow, Rafe cried out, "I am innocent of your blood . . . I would have been your son if—"

"Never," the voice cried out. "It was never meant to be!"

Tears flowed from Rafe's eyes and he sobbed, "Then do with me what you want. . . . Take your revenge and be done with it. . . . These past few days have been harder for me to bear than all my previous years. . . . Everything has been wrong, everything."

"Come with me," the spirit said.

Rafe lifted his head. More frightened than ever, he scrambled backward.

"Come with me," the voice repeated.

"You would take my life for your revenge?" Rafe challenged.

"Come with me," Gumpa's spirit demanded in a thunderous voice that lifted itself against the wild scream of the wind and made the hill quiver. "Time grows short."

Rafe suddenly felt a presence in front of him.

"Extend your hand," the spirit said.

Hesitantly Rafe obeyed the command. He touched something. It was not human, yet it was not a ghost either. A strong hand gripped his and helped him stand. "Where do we go?" he asked.

"There . . . there . . . there," the spirit said.

Before Rafe could ask another question, the flames suddenly flared up and became so high that they seemed to touch the black clouds. He tried to shrink back but the spirit held him where he stood. And before his eyes a place in the wall of flames parted.

He felt himself being moved toward the opening. He fought to free himself. But all his strength was not equal to Gumpa's. Despite the violence of his struggle and his wild screams he was pulled inexorably into the fire. The flames were all around him. But he felt nothing.

"My time is short," the spirit said. "Do not waste it."

As soon as Rafe moved through the opening in the

43

wall of fire, he found himself at the edge of a forest, within sight of a river.

He looked over his shoulder, expecting to see the wall of fire. But it was gone. And in its place were the trackless depths of a forest whose huge evergreens and oaks were lightly dusted with snow.

"Where are we, Gumpa?" he asked, forcing the words out of his fear-constricted throat.

"Back where it began," the spirit answered.

Suddenly Rafe heard sounds. Men shouting to one another in the hard guttural accents of the north and the splash of oars in the river . . . And almost at the same time he saw several men glide noiselessly from tree to tree. He drew back to the protection offered by the stout trunk of a giant oak.

"Though you can see and hear all," Gumpa said, "they are deaf and blind to your presence."

Rafe watched the men move along the edge of the forest. Some were armed with swords, some with spears, and many with battle-axes. They never left the cover of the trees. From his own experience, Rafe knew they were stalking some quarry, ranging like a pack of wolves along the edge of the forest. . . . Since he had become old enough to use a sword, he had taken part in similar raids.

"The ships?" he questioned.

"Yes," the voice replied. "The ships."

Rafe started after the men and was soon in their midst. They were dressed as he was. Suddenly one of them called out in a low voice, "Gumpa, do you think they will come ashore?"

"If they do not," Gumpa answered, "then we will lose them."

Rafe stood very still. He looked at the man who answered to Gumpa's name. He was much younger than the Gumpa he knew.

"It is me as I was," the voice explained. "If you look

44

closely at the other men you will recognize most of them."

"There is Tarki's father," Rafe said, pointing to a thick-set man with long brown hair that flowed out from under his heavy leather helmet. "And Alrek . . . And—"

"Many are here," the spirit said.

"It was Borit's vision we followed. He saw the ships and all they carried. He told me where we would find them."

"What would happen if I touched one of the men?" Rafe questioned.

"He would not feel it," the voice replied.

Once more the voices from the ships and the sounds of the oars drew Rafe's attention from the men in the raiding party to the river where three vessels were easing slowly around a bend. Their huge center sails were furled. The oars flashed in the late-afternoon sun. They were dragon-prowed warships.

A man on the lead vessel shouted to the other men, "We will make camp on the shore for the night." And at his command the vessel turned into the shore. The oarsmen backwatered, waiting for the other two ships to make the turn. And when the three ships were abreast, the order came to bring them to the shore.

The oars dug into the water: one stroke . . . two . . . three . . . four . . . five. And by the sixth stroke the dragon-headed prows simultaneously ground up on the pebble-strewn river bank. Within moments the oars were shipped and the warriors, lifting their shields from the ship's side and their weapons from beneath the rowing benches, leaped ashore ready to fight, should they have to.

More orders were given and stout lines were thrown from the vessels to men on the shore. As soon as the lines were made secure and the ships properly beached, tents and cooking utensils were taken from the vessels. As the camp was being set up, groups of three, four, and six men moved cautiously toward the forest.

Gumpa's men drew back into the depths of the forest. He told them they would strike when most of the warriors were asleep.

Rafe left the forest and walked into the newly made camp. He was surprised to find several women there. One of them was a lovely young woman with olive-brown skin, long black hair, and green eyes. She held a man child in her arms. The other women attended her. She bared her breast and he eagerly sucked the swollen nipple, making loud sounds of contentment.

The woman closed her eyes and, humming softly to herself, she gently stroked the baby's head. Her lovely face was soon suffused with an expression of immense satisfaction.

Rafe went very close to the woman. The air around her was rose-scented. He peered closely at her. He was about to touch her when the voice reminded him that she would feel nothing.

A woman came to her and they spoke in a language unfamiliar to Rafe. The young woman with the child laughed and in Rafe's tongue she slowly said, "One day, when he is a man, he will return to my country and find his destiny there."

"If he sucks like that now," the woman commented, "I pity the poor woman whose breast he mouths when he is a man."

A tall blond gray-eyed warrior came to where the women sat and said to the woman with the child, "Soon we will be finished with the river and after a few days at sea we will reach my stronghold."

Rafe had heard about the sea from men who traveled on the river that flowed past Gumpa's stronghold. In the spring, summer, and fall of the year many ships moved from sea to sea by way of the river and almost all of them paid tribute to Gumpa for the use of his portion of the river. Those few that refused to pay were always attacked and burned. From talking to the oarsmen, Rafe had learned that Gumpa's people and others like them on the river were known as Rus, while the men who came in ships called themselves Vikings. Rafe found it strange that the Rus and the Vikings sacrificed to the same gods and even spoke the same language, though the words sounded strange to his ears when they were spoken by a Viking.

With a nod, the woman said, "It will feel good to remain in one place. This journey has been a difficult one. . . . I hope your lord and my husband will be as kind to me and my child as you and your men have been."

The warrior frowned. "I cannot speak for my king," he told her. "It is not likely he intended to have you bring your bastard whelp to his stronghold, nor is it likely he will feel honored that one of your gods lay with you before he himself did. His gods are Odin, Thor, and the others who live in Asgard, the home of the gods. My king paid your father a goodly amount of gold to have you unused by any other man before he himself bedded with you. But what I tell you does not matter. He will decide the outcome and no one else."

"I understand," the woman answered softly.

Without saying anything else, the warrior moved off, leaving the woman to ponder silently the fate that awaited her and the child at the end of the journey.

Unable to restrain himself, Rafe reached out toward the woman and softly called her mother.

As if she were suddenly chilled, she trembled and drew her cloak more securely around her.

"I told you," the spirit reminded him, "that none you see and hear can see and hear you."

"Will I remember her?" he asked.

"No more than you had before."

"Then why did you bring me to this place?" Rafe cried out. "Why?"

"To show you how it all began," the spirit replied. "To show you the past, so you will know the present and perceive a glimmer of the future."

"What was my mother's name?"

"I do not know," the voice said.

Rafe stayed close to the woman and child. The red glow of the fire in the gathering twilight heightened her beauty. He heard her say to one of the other women, "I feel so peculiar this night."

"Perhaps it is because of the full moon," the woman answered. "On the first night of the full moon, when it hangs low and bright in the sky, the elves come all the way from Alfheim to play tricks on the people who travel through the forests."

"Yes, I know about that," she said with a sigh. "But this is different . . . I feel as though I were here once before. I do not know how that could be—everything here is so familar."

"But how could you have been here? This is more than halfway to the island of Furd."

"There is something close by that knows me," the young woman said, frowning. "I look around me and everything is familiar to me."

"Perhaps your god desires you again."

The young woman shook her head. "Once," she whispered, "and only once."

Neither woman was inclined to speak again and after a while each went to her place to sleep. The encampment was soon still.

Gumpa's spirit directed Rafe's attention to the forest again, where the tops of the trees were silvered with moonlight. "My men are hiding in the branches," the voice said. "But by now they are coming down and they are already positioning themselves for the attack."

Rafe went to the edge of the Viking camp. Guards were posted at intervals all around it and each ship was guarded by two men.

"We come!" the voice exclaimed.

Just as the moon left the sky, the men with Gumpa ran toward the encampment, crouching close to the ground. Suddenly several of them leaped up and the night was alive with arrows.

The Viking guards screamed in agony. More arrows came flying through the moonlit night and more screams filled the night.

The Vikings were up and charging toward their attackers. But sleep still lay heavy on the eyes.

A flight of flame-tipped arrows struck the ships, and fires sprang up on the decks.

Gumpa's raiders were inside the camp. They hacked their way through a line of Viking defenders. Cries to Odin went up from each side, as blade clashed against blade.

Here a man was gutted and there another fell under the crashing blow of a battle-ax.

Shouts and the clang of metal striking metal filled the night air.

Two of the women tried to run toward the forest. One fell under the blow of a battle-ax that carried most of her head away. The other was speared in the back.

Gumpa's attack was directed at the ships. That was where the loot would be: the gold, silver, cloth, and other commodities he and his men would share if the raid was a successful one.

The Vikings fought stubbornly. A group of them made an attempt to launch one of the ships. But Alrek and several others from the stronghold cut them down.

The ground was soon littered with dead and dying men.

Gumpa saw the woman and the child. She was cowering against the side of one of the ships. Smitten by her beauty, he was about to put up his sword and claim her for himself, when Borit suddenly rushed out of the darkness, shouting, "The child is mine. . . . The woman is mine!"

Startled, Gumpa whirled toward Borit.

In that instant the woman drew a knife from her girdle and threw herself on Gumpa, driving the blade into his shoulder. He roared with pain. To be free of her, he threw himself back against the side of the ship.

The woman screamed and released her hold.

Gumpa swung around, caught hold of her, and raised her high above his head.

"Give her to me!" Borit cried.

The woman struggled to free herself.

"Give her to me!" Borit shouted.

"Death shall have her," Gumpa bellowed, and he flung her against the side of the ship. She screamed as she came down. Her head struck the railing and burst open, splattering him with blood.

Turning from the dead woman, Gumpa lifted his sword again and with several of his men he brought to bay those Vikings who had managed to stay alive. The raid was over and many prisoners were taken, including a man child several months old.

"The rest you know," the spirit said to Rafe. "Those I captured, I sacrificed to Odin."

Rafe went to where his mother's body lay crumpled against the side of the vessel. He fought back the tears. All her beauty was gone.

"At first light," Gumpa's spirit said, "I must leave."

"Was my father a god?" Rafe questioned.

"I have heard that gods sometimes lay with mortal men and women," the voice answered. "But such things happen only in places far to the south of where our stronghold is."

"And the king to the north to whom my mother was traveling, what of him?"

"I know nothing about him."

"And my mother's father?"

"Only that he lived in the south," the voice answered.

"Who would know more?" Rafe asked.

"You must find the answer to that question yourself, Rafe. . . . You now know how it began and though it was your spear that killed me, my blood is not on your hands."

"Had I known what you did to my mother," Rafe told him, "I might have tried to kill you long before I did."

"You know the past and the present," the voice said. "The answers are in the future."

"I shall seek them out," Rafe told him. "I shall seek them out, even if it takes my entire life."

"The stars are beginning to fade," Gumpa's spirit said.

Rafe looked up at the sky. The morning star was very bright. The barest hint of dawn was beginning to unravel the night sky. "How will I return to where I was before you led me through the wall of fire?" he asked.

"Do not let anyone stop you," the voice said. "Nothing the gods make happen is without a purpose. . . . Even in death I am not so wise as to know the purpose for all of this but you must find it."

"I will."

"My time has come," Gumpa's spirit said. "My time has come."

The river, the forest, the burning ships, the bodies of the slain and those who had survived the raid—all blurred before Rafe's eyes and melted away into the smoldering embers of Gumpa's funeral pyre.

IX

The wind had dropped off. The snow had stopped falling and in the west the gray twilight sky was streaked with feathery flames.

Rafe was on his knees. The funeral pyre was reduced to ashes. He watched Death lead Gumpa's spirit over the crest of a nearby hill. Though he could not recall what had happened, he felt that something strange and important had occurred.

He stood up, turned, and started down the hill.

Pagar and his brothers ran toward him.

"Your father's spirit has gone with Death," Rafe told them, as they came up to him.

Kinsi said, "We could not see what was happening because of the blowing snow."

Rafe continued to walk.

The people from the stronghold opened their ranks to let him pass. Among them, he caught a glimpse of Astrid.

Pagar joined him on the right, Kinsi on the left. Forra fell in at Kinsi's left.

"How can we be sure what you say is true?" Forra asked. Earlier in the day Borit had called him away from his brothers and told him that Gumpa might reveal to Rafe where he had hidden his treasure of gold and silver. And when Forra had asked why Gumpa would choose to tell his secret to Rafe rather than Pagar, Kinsi, or himself, the priest had said, "Gumpa was strange in his ways and Rafe is more like him than the others."

"It is true," Rafe answered without breaking stride. "I saw Gumpa's spirit walk behind Death just before I left the hill." It was the first time he ever mentioned to anyone he could see Death. But there was no other way for him to have told them.

Kinsi glanced at Forra and for a moment tried to look past Rafe to Pagar. "Not many men see Death during their lifetime," he commented.

"I have seen him many times," Rafe said with a sigh. His experience with Gumpa's spirit, whatever it was, had tired him more than he had realized.

"You saw my father's spirit?" Forra questioned.

"Only when he was with Death."

"Where?"

Rafe gestured toward the distant hill and said, "Going over the crest there."

"Why should you be able to see Death?" Kinsi asked.

"I do not know," Rafe answered.

By the time they reached the stronghold's gate, the gray twilight had deepened into darkness. That Rafe claimed to have the power to see Death made Gumpa's sons uneasy. They had previously been warned by Borit to expect Rafe to exaggerate his prowesses. The priest had cautioned the three of them to be disingenuous toward him. . . .

"Accept what he tells you without argument," Borit said, letting his gray eyes move from one to the other. "Long before Gumpa took him from the fire, he was given two destinies; one would have seen him consumed by the flames and the other would have him kill the man who had saved him from Death; then be captured by the sons of the murdered man and given by them to the gods. By taking him from the fire,

Gumpa not only assured his own death but also gave Rafe his second destiny."

"But why have the gods waited so long?" Pagar asked.

"They do not wait for anything. Only man waits. What to us is twenty years is but a moment to them. I have seen them work their mysteries many, many times."

Gumpa's sons thanked the priest and returned to their vigil at the base of the hill. . . .

"What did he want?" Pagar asked, breaking his long silence.

Rafe shook his head.

"Gumpa must have told you something," Kinsi said.

"His spirit called me; I went to him and now he is with Death. I cannot tell you more."

"You mean you *will* not!" Forra exclaimed angrily. He darted out ahead of Kinsi and, coming in front of Rafe, he forced him to stop. "I do not know about Kinsi or Pagar," he said, "but I for one do not believe you."

"It is of no matter to me whether you believe me," Rafe responded. "I did you and your brothers a service. I did not expect to return but the old woman needed rest and—"

"You were alone," Pagar reminded him.

"I am sure I will find her," Rafe said with a shrug.

"You came alone," Kinsi said.

Rafe realized then that all of the people from the stronghold had trooped after them. From the way they looked at him, he could sense their hostility.

"I say," Forra announced in a loud voice, "that if you spoke to my father, you should be able to tell us what he said."

Kinsi agreed with his younger brother. Then some of the other men from the stronghold sided with them.

"I remember nothing of what happened," Rafe told them. "It was like a dream that passes on waking."

"I think you take me and my brothers for fools," Forra replied hotly.

"He takes no one for a fool," Borit said, coming out of the darkness near the palisade. He walked with measured step to where the four men stood. Across his shoulders he wore the red mantle of his calling and in his right hand he carried his ashwood staff. "I have seen other men," Borit commented, "who could not remember what they experienced with a spirit. . . . It is not uncommon. . . . For some the memory of such an encounter is enough to make them lose their wits completely."

Forra was somewhat mollified and stepped aside, muttering to himself that he would rather have the matter settled sooner than later.

Rafe thanked the priest, though he was surprised that he interceded on his behalf. In the past, Borit had never shown him the slightest interest. And he was sure his expulsion from the stronghold had been the result of the priest's communion with the gods.

"I want you to rest this night with me," Borit said, "before you continue your journey."

Rafe looked toward Pagar and said, "Will you honor your father's word and allow me to rest? Tomorrow I will be gone and you can begin your hunt."

"I say we take him now," Forra growled.

"What is your word on this, Kinsi?" Pagar asked.

"I will honor Gumpa's word," Kinsi answered.

Borit's narrow lips cracked into a smile. "Come," he said to Rafe. "I have a good fire . . . some cabbage in a pot and, best of all, some quantity of mead left in one of my jars."

Rafe followed him. But his stride soon put him at the priest's side. "I will be glad to eat and drink," he said. "I am very hungry and very tired."

Together they entered the stronghold and walked to the far end, near the river where Borit lived. "Tell me," the priest said as they entered his house, "do you really remember nothing of your experience with Gumpa's spirit?"

"Nothing," Rafe answered as he stooped to get past the doorway.

"Well," Borit said, and going to the hearth, he stirred the ashes to fire, "perhaps I can help you remember. . . . Sometimes mead or any strong drink works miracles in that direction. Unless of course you are afraid."

"I am not afraid," Rafe answered.

Borit smiled thinly but did not speak.

Pagar now occupied the large oaken chair at the head of the table. On his right sat Kinsi and to his left was Forra. The day had been long and tiring. All of the young ones were already asleep and though the women were still at their table, most of them were readying themselves to retire for the night.

Pagar had never before realized how huge the chair was, nor how big a man his father had been. The chair, with its high back carved at the top into an eagle, made him feel considerably smaller than he was.

"The chair," he said in a low voice, "will take getting used to."

Kinsi nodded.

And Forra said, "Since you are our chieftain, I will tell you that I think you must not wait to get used to anything, be it Gumpa's chair, or any of his women, or doing what must be done." He made no attempt to mask his passion. He had spent most of the evening thinking about what to say and now that he had said it, he waited for his brother's response.

"A yearling cannot be a three-year-old," Kinsi commented with a laugh. "Give him time—"

"He will only grow if he acts," Forra said with a vigorous shaking of his head.

"Tonight he will act with one of the women. . . . Which one will it be, Pagar?"

"Forra has something else in mind," Pagar said.

"Indeed I have," the youngest of Gumpa's sons answered.

"Have your say," Pagar told him.

"We know our father was less than open about his possessions, especially when it came to gold and silver. Much of what he took on his raids lies buried somewhere. Perhaps it is in a cave in the rock cliffs that are on the river to the north. It might even be closer than that—somewhere inside or nearby the stronghold." Forra shifted his eyes from Pagar to Kinsi and then back to Pagar again, before he said, "Gumpa never had the chance to reveal where he had hidden his store of gold and silver."

"Had he stored food," Pagar responded, "then it would be worth every man's effort to search for it. . . . Now . . . Now—" he hesitated for a few moments then added, "Now my people need food not gold and silver."

"Gold and silver can buy food," Kinsi said, looking at his younger brother with new respect. Pagar was without a doubt the best hunter among them but he certainly was not the most quick-witted or the shrewdest.

"Gold and silver can buy anything," Forra told them. "We can buy meat and grain from the people who live in Miklagard."

Pagar nodded.

Forra uttered a deep sigh of relief before he said, "In a matter of weeks we can have food here."

"Yes, that is true," Pagar responded. "But it might take us weeks, perhaps even longer, to find the gold and silver. . . . Where would we begin to look for it?

You yourself said it could be in a cave, here in the stronghold or someplace nearby."

"It will be easier than that," Forra answered. "The gods have made it much easier."

"I do not understand how."

Kinsi was smiling broadly.

Forra looked at him and smiled. "You tell him," he told his brother.

"The gods have given us Rafe," Kinsi responded.

"And what Gumpa told him," Forra said, "he will tell us."

Pagar pulled on his beard. He did not understand how a man who remembered nothing of what had happened to him could possibly reveal the location of a hidden treasure and he told his brothers as much, adding, "Besides, neither of you can be sure that Gumpa told him anything at all."

"He had to tell him something," Kinsi said, exasperated by Pagar's dullness.

"Tell me, brother," Forra challenged, "what do you think happened up there on the top of the hill?"

"I do not know."

"Gumpa would speak to no one else but Rafe," Forra said, his face now dark red with anger. "What could be more important than—"

"What Forra is trying to say," Kinsi broke in, "is that Gumpa revealed the location of his treasure to Rafe."

"But why him? Why not one of us?"

"Why not indeed!" exclaimed Forra, suddenly crashing his balled fist down on the table with such force that it made the bowls leap up. Then he was on his feet. The torchlight served only to make his already flushed face more red. He placed his palms on the table and leaned over it, while looking at his older brother. "Because he favored him more than you, more than Kinsi there or more than me."

Pagar shifted uneasily in the massive chair. "There

is no need for you to be disrespectful to Gumpa." His voice was hard.

"I am only saying what is true. . . . He favored Rafe; everyone in the stronghold knows that. If it were not for the fact that we all know he took him in a raid, he might have fathered him on some strange woman, they were so much alike."

"If that was so, why did Gumpa send him away?" Pagar asked, leaning forward. His blood had begun to run hot too.

"Because the gods willed it. . . . Borit told him the gods willed it. But even with that Gumpa would not yield him up. Even with the gods demanding Rafe, our father saw fit to give him the chance to escape the flames. He would go to the fire only if we caught him. . . ." Forra was breathing heavily and even though it was cold enough in the great hall to make steam of his breath, his brow was wet with sweat. "Did it ever occur to you, Pagar, that you, Kinsi, or I might be killed by Rafe while hunting him?"

"I have thought about it," Kinsi said quietly.

Pagar nodded but did not speak.

"If Gumpa was willing to risk any one of us for him, which of us did he love more, Rafe or his sons?"

Pagar remained silent. Out of the corner of his left eye he watched the women finally leave the table.

"It was Rafe's spear that killed Gumpa," Kinsi reminded them.

"Borit left no doubt about who killed Gumpa," Forra said. "Yet Gumpa wanted to speak only to him. . . . The reason has to be that he wanted to tell him something very important. And I cannot think of anything more important than to know where a treasure has been hidden."

"Why would he tell Rafe?"

"Because," Kinsi said, "of all the things Forra has been telling you."

"And possibly two more," Forra told him. "Gumpa could not have known who killed him. Second, by providing Rafe with the secret of his treasure Gumpa might have hoped that with the gold and silver he would be able to buy his life from us and avoid being given to the gods altogether. . . . If any man knew what gold and silver could buy, Gumpa was that man."

"If as you say, he had this treasure," Pagar asked, "what prevented him from using it to buy food as you would have me do?"

"He was your father as well as mine," Forra answered. "But had we been closer, I might have asked him."

Pagar rubbed his short brown beard. And after a while, he asked, "How do we speak to Rafe about this?"

"A fire on the soles of his feet will bring forth Gumpa's secret," Forra answered.

"Then you would torture him?"

"I would flay him alive to find out where Gumpa hid his gold and silver."

"And you, Kinsi," Pagar asked, "how do you stand?"
"With Forra."

"And I say," Forra said, "That we take him tonight . . . that we do not give him the chance to escape, for with his escape will go our opportunity to find Gumpa's gold and silver."

"Tomorrow morning will be time enough to take him," Pagar said.

"Then we will force the secret from him?" Forra asked.

"If it must be done that way," Pagar said, "it will be. . . . But I will offer him his life for it. Then if he refuses to tell us where the treasure is, he will suffer a long and hard torture and be given to the gods."

"A wise decision!" Forra exclaimed, heartily gripping his brother's right hand.

"We will all be the better for it," Kinsi said, placing his right hand over the clasped hands of his brothers.

Pagar was pleased with himself and, yawning, he said he was tired and would enjoy a good sleep.

Kinsi nudged him in the ribs with his elbow and told him, "You will work harder with a woman than you had all day."

"Ah, but that will be pleasure," Pagar laughed, "and hardly any work at all."

The three brothers laughed long and hard.

Much later, when only a few torches continued to burn and those only feebly, Kinsi moved quietly to where Forra slept. Placing his hand across his brother's mouth lest he should cry out, he called softly to him.

Forra opened his eyes.

Kinsi removed his hand from Forra's mouth. "You showed a side of yourself I did not see before," he whispered.

"It was time to reveal it," Forra answered, propping himself up on his elbow.

Kinsi gestured toward where Pagar slept and said, "He will never fit into Gumpa's chair."

Forra nodded.

"One of us should sit there," Kinsi said.

"In time one of us will," Forra responded. "In time one of us will. . . ."

X

Rafe had never before been in the priest's house, much less sat at his table. He was uncertain of his feelings. Though he was thankful for shelter and the prospect of food and drink, he was wary of the man who had always remained aloof from him and had served as the messenger of the gods to Gumpa when they had demanded his sacrifice. The house, though it consisted of one large room divided into a place for sleeping and a place to cook and eat, was warm and free from drafts. The walls were stone and the sharply pitched roof was made of split logs, laid over with river clay to fill in the cracks and many heavy stones to hold it down when the wind blew hard.

Borit spooned out a large bowl of cabbage leaves and set it down in front of Rafe. "There is more if you are still hungry after you have finished this," he said.

Using the blade of his knife to cut and spear the smaller pieces of cabbage, he began to eat voraciously; now and then lifting the bowl to his lips to drink the broth. He found the leaves and the broth more satisfying than he had thought possible. Other times he had eaten boiled cabbage but never before had it made him feel he was eating meat.

"It is in the spices I used," Borit said, when Rafe asked him about the meatlike flavor. And he poured a cup of mead for his guest.

Rafe indulged himself and asked for another bowl of cabbage. Only when he was almost finished with it did he realize that Borit neither ate nor drank. Ashamed for having gorged himself at his host's table, he said apologetically, "I was far hungrier than I realized.

"And far more thirsty," Borit said with a slight laugh, pouring more mead into Rafe's cup. "I also use special herbs when I brew this," he explained. "That is why it is darker than ordinary mead and somewhat sweeter."

Nodding, Rafe drank all of the mead and told the priest, "I am grateful to you. Though I have had much more elaborate fare, I will never forget your kindness."

"Well said," Borit responded zestfully. "Very well said."

Rafe's eyes moved from the priest to the battle-ax and shield on the far wall.

"The ax," Borit said, noticing where his guest was looking, "is made of good bronze and will hold edge for a long time. The shield is made of the same metal and offers fine protection. You can see, even from where you are, several places where it took the blows from other weapons."

The priest had some renown as a fighter. It was often said by the men in the stronghold that had he not become a priest, he would have been one of Gumpa's best warriors.

He left the table and, going to where the arms were hung, he ran the forefinger of his right hand straight down from the top of the shield. "That was a blow from a sword taken in a raid a long time ago on some Viking ships that were returning to Miklagard," he explained, choosing his words very carefully to see what effect they would have on his guest. "I fought with a man who was guarding a woman and child."

"The blow must have been a mighty one to make a crease like that," Rafe answered.

"It almost felled me," the priest said, going back to the table. "But it was I who struck the man down."

Rafe yawned. He was having difficulty keeping his eyes open. The room seemed to have become warmer.

"For tonight," the priest said, "you may use the extra sleeping pallet."

Rafe stood up and staggered over to where several skin robes lay over some rough-hewn planks. "This will do fine," he said, sinking down on the pallet with a sigh. "My head suddenly feels very, very large."

Borit laughed and told him, 'The mead was stronger than you suspected."

"Perhaps . . . perhaps . . . perhaps."

The priest went closer to his guest to be sure he was asleep. Nodding with satisfaction, he moved to the hearth, where he dropped several chips of stone in the fire. The flames leaped high; their red changed to purple and from this arose a black vapor.

Borit extended his hands toward the raven-hued mist and beckoned it to him. It drew back, clinging in the back of the hearth like some loathsome creature from the dark world of Hel.

The priest responded by incanting a prayer, to his lord and master, the God of Darkness. "Give me the strength to do your will," he implored. "Let me have mastery over this spirit so I may mold it to your designs." Once again he held his hands toward the black mist and summoned it to him with his long fingers. It clung even more fiercely to the rear stones of the hearth.

"Grant me the power," he cried out. "Grant your humble servant his request." Within moments the fingers on Borit's hands became claws; then leaping into the midst of the purple flames, he tore the black vapor from the stones and hurled it on the floor in front of the hearth where, shrieking, it attempted to slither back into the flames from whence it sprung. But it was not fast enough to escape the priest, who rushed from the flames and, grabbing hold of the swirling black vapor with his clawlike hands, quickly shaped it into a human form and then into a woman.

"Hear me," Borit ordered. "Hear your master and obey his word."

The blackness turned to cold, gray ashes and with the voice of a woman, it answered, "I will do all you command."

Borit turned toward the pallet where Rafe slept. "Go to him," he said. "Envelop him with your lust so that in his lust he will reveal all that took place between him and the spirit of Gumpa. . . . Then come and tell me."

The specter loosed a high-pitched laugh.

"Tell me all he tells you," Borit commanded.

"Yes, master," the spirit answered. "But in whose form should I come to him?"

Borit considered the question. He could not risk using Astrid's likeness again, lest Rafe discover, as he previously had, the spirit's true nature, and so he told the wraith, "He is young and lusty. Assume a form that would please him."

Pointing to Rafe, the priest said, "Now go and do my bidding."

The phantom drifted across the floor. As it drew closer to Rafe, it became more defined, gaining the beauty of a living woman. Bending over him, it blew gently into his ear.

Rafe stirred.

She blew again, this time whispering his name.

In his dreams Rafe was mounted on a magnificent white stallion. He rode through a forest until he reached a place where the trees gave way to a grassy glen. He dismounted and as he started to lead his horse to the glade, he saw her. She was sitting on a large flat rock near a slow-flowing creek, next to her a piebald palfrey.

She smiled at him.

He moved closer. She was a beautiful woman with eyes that matched the color of her long black hair.

"I am riding north," he told her, "and stopped to rest my horse."

"And I too am resting here," she answered.

Rafe released the reins to let his horse graze. He glanced up at the sky. The tops of the trees were high and very dark against the sky. A strange silence hung over the land. Nothing moved. No bird sang or fluttered from branch to branch. No frog croaked or leaped with a splash into the nearby creek. And not a leaf stirred from the caress of a vagrant breeze.

"Where is this place?" Rafe asked.

"Not far from my father's great hall," the woman answered.

The closer Rafe got to her, the more beautiful the woman became. The air around her was perfumed. . . . Then suddenly she was in his arms. Her firm high breasts pressed hard against his chest. Within moments they were naked, each caressing the other's body.

"I would know your heart," she told him in a breathy voice, "as well as your body."

Such pleasure came from her touch that he could only stammer, "I ride north."

"But why north?"

And before Rafe could answer he saw, from out of the corner of his right eye, a patch of land beyond the glade. The ground there was barren and parched. He stirred, lifting himself from her body.

"No, no!" the woman exclaimed and clutched him fiercely to her.

He bent his head to the pink nipples of her breasts and sucked each one between his lips.

"Ah," she moaned, moving her head from side to side in a counterfeit of real pleasure. "Ah, you fill my body with fire."

Rafe was about to answer, when all at once the forest vanished. In a second dream he was standing on the parched, rocky plain he had previously seen. A hot red sun glowed in the dark sky. Two figures came close to him. One was a man, the other a woman. The man was dressed in black. The woman was in white.

"I claim him," the man shouted.

"He will be mine," the woman answered.

Their voices filled the space between the earth and the sky; his like thunder and hers like the roar of the river at full flood.

"I will bed with you," the man bellowed. "Your body and mine will combine to bring forth a race of demons to people the world."

"Never," the woman answered. "Never . . . He will come to me."

The man sprung at the woman.

She eluded him.

He caught up to her and tore the gown from her body. Her nakedness drove him to a fury of passion.

But she fought him off.

The earth trembled beneath them. The sky above them blackened.

"Wake," she cried. "Wake, Rafe, before it is too late. And flee—flee before it is too late."

The instant he heard his name, the figures vanished. The red sun dissolved, dripping blood across the sky. . . .

Rafe sought the body of the raven-haired woman. But she became less and less substantial until she vanished from his dream.

He blinked and was awake. Except for the light

that came from a low-burning torch and the glowing embers of the fire, the room was dark. Suddenly he saw something slithering along the floor. Grabbing his sword, he leaped to his feet and went after it. But it moved too fast and as it escaped into the flames, the wind in the chimney cried out, "He rides north. . . . He rides north. . . ."

Rafe turned toward Borit. The priest was asleep at the table with his head resting on his arms.

Without thinking about what he was doing, Rafe hastened to the door and opened it just wide enough for him to squeeze through. Once he was in the cold night air, he was careful to close it quietly, lest he wake Borit.

Moments later he was running across the frozen river toward the forest that lay close to the far bank. Rafe wanted to be well away from the stronghold by the time morning came.

XI

Borit raised the alarm, shouting, "Rafe is gone. . . . Rafe has escaped. . . . Rafe has run away." He charged through the stronghold toward Pagar's hall and when he reached it, he battered on the door with his fist, still raising a hue and cry.

Kinsi rushed for the door. Forra went after him. Pagar called for his men to light the torches. Here and there children began to cry.

The door was opened and a sudden gush of wind bent the flames of the torches away from the door.

Pagar was now with his two younger brothers.

"He is gone," Borit shouted at them. "Rafe has escaped!"

Forra and Kinsi ran back to their sleeping pallets for their arms. Within moments they were back with Borit and Pagar.

"How could he have gotten away?" Kinsi asked.

"I mixed a special sleeping potion," Borit explained. "I even cast a spell over him to bind him where he lay."

"You told me," Forra fumed, "that he would be there this morning. We could have held him here in the hall with good rope, far better than you have managed with your draughts and spells."

Pagar silenced his youngest brother with a wave of his hand. "We will go after him," he said. "He is on foot. There is snow on the ground. We will take our

horses. It should not be difficult to capture him. . . ."
Then as an afterthought, he added, "We will hunt him
as Gumpa would had done had he lived. . . . The
four of us will take three men each. Forra, you ride
south. Kinsi ride east—"

"He has gone north," Borit said.

"How do you know that?" Forra questioned, his anger unabated.

Glowering at him, Borit lied, "Because of my spell
he could not leave without first telling me the direction he intended to take."

"Had only your spell been strong enough to also
make him tell you where he was going," Forra responded sarcastically. "Or better still, where we might
find Gumpa's gold and silver!"

"You should have stopped him," Kinsi said to the
priest.

Borit frowned. These men were fools. He was sorely
tempted to kill all of them. With his god's help, he
could do it with a wave of his hand, or if death was
too strong a punishment he could easily change the
three of them into braying asses. But he controlled his
anger, knowing that what he would do Inanna, the
goddess of life would undo. Besides, he still had a use
for Pagar and his brothers. "I would have stopped
him," the priest said. "But he moved too quickly for
me."

Forra snorted with disdain.

"Arguing here about what should have been done,"
Pagar told them, "accomplishes nothing more than in-
creasing everyone's ire. . . . Kinsi, pick your men. . . .
You too, Forra. . . . Borit, you will ride with me. . . .
I want every man to carry his sword and spear."

Forra and Kinsi retreated inside the hall and began
calling out the names of the men who would accom-
pany them.

"I want to take Rafe alive," Pagar said to Borit.

71

With a nod, the priest answered, "Alive, the gods will have what they want and you and your brothers will be able to learn the hiding place of Gumpa's treasure."

A short while later, Pagar led some fifteen horsemen across the frozen river to the far bank, where they fanned out and began their search. Forra was the first to call out that he had found Rafe's footprints in the snow. But no sooner did Pagar and Kinsi gallop to where he was, than another man shouted that he came upon Rafe's footprints. And yet a third man called that he found the footprints. Within a matter of moments calls came from various other riders that they had seen the footprints.

Before anyone realized what was happening, tempers flared. Harsh words were exchanged and weapons came into play. Sword clanged against sword. Some of the men dueled with spears.

Pagar shouted to the men to stop. But each claimed the right to defend the honor of his find. Blood stained the white snow.

"Stop them," Pagar shouted to Borit. "Call upon the gods to stop them."

"Fools," the priest shouted, "they are fools." And waving his right hand from south to north and back again, he brought a howling wind down on them, filled the sky with laden clouds, and pulled the snow down from them.

Regardless of the sudden storm that swept over them, the men continued to fight. More and more fell wounded, or were killed by their neighbor's weapon.

A sword was thrust into Forra's chest and, dropping to his knees, he vomited blood. Kinsi was run through with a spear. And Pagar was forced to hack his way to the frozen river, killing many of the men who would have served him loyally under other circumstances, as they had served Gumpa for so many years.

Though the hubbub of the slaughter raged about him, Borit remained safe inside the magic circle he had inscribed around himself in the snow with the point of his sword. He watched the carnage with disdain, while from a distant place the very wind he had conjured brought the sound of Inanna's mocking laughter.

"I will win in the end," he shouted, whirling his sword wildly over his head. "I will have you for my own!"

The taunting laughter continued.

Borit was furious that so many years of waiting had brought him nothing. He implored his god to help him wreak his vengeance and pointed his sword at Pagar. Almost at once the ice cracked and then gave way under Gumpa's eldest son, plunging him and his horse to their doom in the cold depths of the river.

Then spurring his own mount, the priest galloped forward. The earth trembled as his horse crashed through the magic circle. Leaving the dead and the dying behind him on the blood-drenched snow, he and his steed raced into the depths of the forest. Now there was no longer any reason for him to remain Borit. As he galloped through the forest, he discarded his priestly mantle. Once more he became Enlil, the son of Bal begotten on the body of Lilith, a mortal woman. Half man, half demon!

"You have gained nothing, Inanna, but time," he shouted. "In the end I will kill Rafe and then claim you."

Her laughter followed him. . . .

Rafe ran until he felt his chest would burst and then sucking in great draughts of air he continued to run.

The darkness faded. Dawn came: first a gray, then a light pink that spread across the eastern sky until the first arc of the yellow sun showed itself above the horizon.

Finally, Rafe could run no more. Every part of his body ached with weariness. Gaining the top of a small rise, he flung himself down. Sweat blurred his vision and he felt light-headed, as if he had drunk too much mead.

He gasped for breath and, rolling onto his back, he looked up at a lovely azure sky. The sun was warm on his face. He closed his eyes and silently told himself that even if every man in the stronghold were coming at him, he would not be able to move.

"I want nothing more than to sleep," he mumbled. "Nothing more than to sleep."

Rafe slept and in his sleep he found himself once more in that dry country beyond the forest. He recognized the place because the earth was brown, huge boulders were close by, and the sun was pouring fire over the land.

Then a voice, a woman's voice that came from nowhere and everywhere at once, said, "Seek your destiny and you will find me."

Rafe awoke with a start. The moment his eyes were open he saw Talum. She was seated no more than a pace away from him.

Her lips were parted in a toothless grin. Alternately she shook and nodded her skull-like head.

"How long have you been sitting here?" he asked, sitting up. His body still ached.

"Since before you came," she answered.

"I did not see you. But if I had, I would have chosen some other place to rest," he answered, still angry at her for the trick she had played on him the previous morning.

She clicked her tongue, saying nonchalantly, "I have been waiting here for you."

74

Rafe snorted with disdain. "Had you not fled," he told her, "you would not have had to wait. . . . I told Gumpa's sons you were with me and not only were you gone but you managed to take your footprints with you."

Cackling with glee, Talum said, "It is not difficult to do once you have learned how. . . . It is more difficult though to become a crow and speak like a human being, while appearing to speak like a crow."

Rafe did not answer.

"Did you know that I and the crow were one and the same?" she asked, looking at him with her old black eyes bright and shiny with mirth.

"Witch woman," he replied, "I do not know people who become crows, or take their footprints with them when they vanish or—" Suddenly he began to smile. "It was not funny," he said, but nonetheless, he began to laugh. Soon he was guffawing. He shook his head and held his aching sides.

"But what you said," she told him, when his laughter diminished, "is not entirely true."

"I know no other witch woman, or man for that matter," he replied.

"But you yourself can see Death," she said.

Rafe nodded, though puzzled by what she was trying to tell him.

"And sometimes, you are even able to understand the language of birds and animals."

"That is no more than any hunter can do," he replied.

"There is understanding and there is a deeper form of understanding. . . . Yours is the second kind."

"Tell me what you want to," he said. "I have no patience for guessing at your meaning."

"Things that you do few other men can. . . . The powers you possess are special."

75

"I have no powers," he said. "If I had, would I be here? Would I have been driven from my people, from the stronghold?"

"They are not your people," Talum told him in a low voice.

He did not reply.

"Come," she said, "we must not tarry here too long."

Rafe waved her comment aside. "I will travel alone," he told her. "Even now I am being hunted by the men from the stronghold. Besides, after what you did to me, I see no reason why I should burden myself with an old crone. Wherever I go, I would be much better off without you." And scrambling to his feet, he started down the slope.

Talum went after him.

He was surprised at the swiftness of her movements. She was at his side before the top of his head went below the crest of the hillock.

"You need not fear the men from the stronghold," she told him.

"Not now," he answered, quickening his pace. "But should they catch me, I would have every reason to fear them."

She grabbed hold of his arm and stayed his movement.

He tried to free himself but could not. She was stronger by far than he or any other man could ever hope to be.

"Fear only Borit," she said. "All the others do not matter. But he whose fate is linked to yours will not rest until it is decided which of you shall have Inanna."

Rafe shook himself free, not because his strength finally triumphed but rather because the crone relaxed her hold on his arm. He was about to speak when suddenly all that had just taken place on the snow-covered river bank across from the stronghold flashed like a blaze of lightning before his eyes. He saw it and then it was gone.

"But how could something like that happen?" he asked. And before she could answer, he added, "I do not know Inanna and never have. Besides, what has she to do with all of this?"

"The last question first," Talum said. "You will know the answer when you find her. The first question next. They were dead only to Borit's eyes. They have already awakened with no memory of the fight. As to whether or not you know Inanna, it is never possible for a person to say who they really know or do not know. But to stop you from racking your brain over Inanna, I will tell you that you do not know her."

"Witch woman," Rafe told her harshly, "I want neither your answers nor company." And he walked away from her.

She came after him, saying, "Borit is your enemy, not me."

"Borit has never been a friend but he is surely not an enemy. Why, just last night he gave me food and shelter."

"And drink?"

"Yes, mead . . . Wonderfully spiced mead."

"And he was generous because he was neither your enemy nor your friend?"

"When you speak of it," Rafe answered, "you twist my words to make them sound foolish to my own ears."

Ignoring his question, she asked, "What made you run from his house?"

He started to speak but stopped himself before he said something foolish.

"A voice?" she suggested. "Remember the voice that warned you to run, to flee before it was too late?"

"You?" he questioned.

"Inanna," she answered.

Rafe shook his head. He was wasting his time talking to her. He began to walk again.

Talum went along with him. "Think on this," she said. "The contest is between Enlil, whom you know as Borit, and Inanna. You are the prize."

"If I were to devote thought to what you have just told me," he said, snapping his fingers, "I would be wasting my time. . . . I do not want to hear any more about Inanna or Enlil or even Borit."

The crone did not answer.

But every so often as they hurried along, Rafe glanced at her out of the corner of his eye. He did not believe her stories about Inanna and Enlil and if it were not that he feared her magic, he most certainly would have begun to run again. . . .

XII

Rafe and Talum followed the river north, though for the sake of safety during the day they kept to the cover offered by the trees of the forest and only went to the river bank at night when they camped. They progressed slowly. The crone was more of a burden than Rafe had thought she would be. Often when she tired and he was too impatient to stop to rest, he carried her on his back.

At such times, she would pretend he was a horse, kick him with her heels, and shout, "Ho there, go faster . . . Faster I tell you!" Or if she did not use her heels, she always managed to find a switch and use the branch liberally on his rump.

Once while she was on his shoulders and swatted him harder than usual, he unceremoniously dumped her on the ground.

The fall took her breath away and brought tears to her eyes.

Rafe stood by and laughed; then shaking his finger at her, he said, "I will do that whenever you mistake me for a horse."

Talum scrambled to her feet and complained that he was mistreating an old woman.

"Do I kick or use a switch on you?" he questioned.

"How else am I to speed you on your way?" she replied.

"I could go a lot faster if I did not have to wait for you, or carry you," he told her.

And so they walked side by side, arguing about the matter; she maintaining that her actions kept him moving and he telling her that he could move faster if he did not have her to slow him down. But when she complained of being tired again, he lifted her on his shoulders and carried her until twilight came and they camped for the night on the bank of the river.

Traveling most of the day and making camp early became a pattern. When they sat close to the small fire and ate what roots they could dig up, they seldom spoke. Usually Rafe would wait until the crone was asleep before he stretched out and let sleep come to him. But sometimes he would ask her questions about Inanna and Enlil, especially Enlil, since he was supposed to be his enemy.

One evening, he asked, "But why did Enlil wait so long to attempt to kill me, when he could have done it so many other times?"

Talum stirred the ashes with a small stick. Then she said, "He could not do it. Even for him there are rules and he must abide by them, or meet with the displeasure of the other gods and forfeit his claim to Inanna."

"Are you telling me that Borit—or as you call him, Enlil—is a god?" Rafe asked, shaking his head doubtfully.

"He is part god. . . . Bal is his father and his mother was a mortal woman. But his lord and master is Urd, the God of Darkness and Chaos."

"But with such power as his, Enlil could have killed me long ago," Rafe protested.

Talum shook her head and told him, "It is not for you to question the gods."

Rafe did not pursue the conversation. The crone would not tell him any more than she already had. And so he silently stared into the flames, waiting for her to go to sleep so that he might stretch out and sleep too.

Despite his annoyance with Talum, Rafe soon found himself oddly attached to her. And if she would wander off for too long a time, he would raise a shout until he saw her again. Her presence made him wonder about his own mother. He was too young when Gumpa took him captive to remember anything about her. Yet more often than not she was in his thoughts. Several nights running, the dreams that came to him when he slept were full of violent actions. Once he saw Gumpa lead his men out of the forest; another time there were Vikings bringing three ships in to shore and then the three vessels burst into flames; and almost always he saw an olive-skinned woman with long black hair.

Then one night he saw the olive-skinned woman being raised in the air and thrown against the side of a ship. He cried out and awoke with a start.

Talum bolted up.

"Go back to sleep, old woman," Rafe told her. "An ugly dream visited me."

"You have been whimpering in your sleep for several nights," she said.

He looked down at the embers.

"Braver and stronger men than you," she commented, "have been afraid of their dreams."

"I am not afraid of them," Rafe answered.

"Then what bothers you so, if it is not fear?"

"My mother," he explained softly. "I dream about my mother." And lifting his eyes from the glow of the embers to the crone's face, he said, "I never knew her."

The crone said nothing.

Rafe stretched out again and stared at the stars until his eyelids fell shut. But the next morning, instead of leaving the river bank and going into the forest, he moved along the river.

Talum made no mention of the change.

Rafe increased his pace, sometimes breaking into a run.

The crone, lagging behind him, complained of the pace.

He went back to her and, hunkering, he said, "Come, climb on my shoulders and I will carry you. . . . But no kicking with your heels or using the switch." He waited till she was settled and then began to run.

"Where are you going in such a hurry?" she asked.

Without answering, Rafe continued to jog. Something was pulling at him. He could feel it but he could not put into words what he felt.

Morning passed and most of the afternoon went by before he slowed down. "It is close," he said. "Very close." He stopped and, easing the crone off of his shoulders, he went to the river to drink.

"How much farther do we have to go?" she asked.

He came up the bank and, taking hold of her hand, he said, "Beyond the bend there." And lifting Talum to her feet, he led the crone after him.

Already the sun was low in the west and the shadows on the forest were quickly weaving twilight's gray cloak.

Rafe slowed and then stopped. He stood very still. Before him lay the bend in the river. His heart skipped a beat and then began to race. Though he had drunk his fill of water, his lips were dry and his throat felt like rough stone. He let go of the crone's hand and slowly started to walk.

Talum followed some distance behind him.

He did not go with the river. Instead, he crossed the spit of land that formed the bow. He was sweating and his breath formed puffs of steam in the cold air.

He stopped and in a distant voice, he said, "Talum, I know this place . . . I have been here before."

"What do you know?" she asked.

He began to walk again. "There," he said, "the burnt-out hulks of the three ships." He ran to them. "Here . . . here," he cried out. "Here are the bones of the Vikings who died fighting. . . ." He scrambled from fire-blackened remains to fire-blackened remains. Little was left of the once proud ships. A few charred timbers, a few ribs. "Here my mother was killed," he shouted. "In this place she was dashed against the ship."

Talum came to his side and gently took hold of his hand.

"I know this place," he shouted, looking up at the night sky, where the first few stars were brightly glowing. "I remember all of it. . . . There by the side of the first ship was my mother. I was in her arms when—Borit came. He claimed me and then her. But Gumpa—she tries to fight him; Gumpa lifts her up and—"

"Come," Talum said softly but firmly. "Come!"

Rafe allowed himself to be led away. Much later when they were seated at the fire, he asked her if she knew who he was.

"You will know that," she answered, "when you discover it for yourself."

"Do you know who my mother was?"

"Only that she was a beautiful woman."

"Did you ever see her?"

"In dreams as you have," Talum answered.

"But why should you—"

Holding up her long-fingered hand to silence him, she said, "Find the answer to who and what you are and you will have the answers to everything else." Then she moved away from the fire and lay down to sleep.

Rafe remained awake long into the night thinking about his mother; then he too slept. . . .

Not too many days after Rafe and Talum left the place where Gumpa had killed Rafe's mother, a gentle warmth settled on the land. Spring had finally come. The snow melted quickly and almost overnight the trees were full of green buds and slender blades of grass speared their way out of the dark earth.

Rafe saw signs of game. He was able to snare a rabbit or a bird to eat each night. He never failed to share equally with Talum whatever game he managed to take. But since his experience at the bend in the river where the Viking ships had been burned, he had become even more reticent than before.

Often they traveled whole days without speaking. Rafe returned to his former practice of moving through the forest during the day and camping for the night at the river bank.

The buds on the trees soon became a filigree of small leaves and Talum remarked they looked like delicate lace.

"I do not know what this is," Rafe said with a shake of his head.

"It is a woman's cloth," she told him. "But it is seldom seen by the Rus, though some trade it to the Vikings when they can get it from the south."

"And how would you know about it?" he questioned.

She replied with a cackle but did not augment it with words.

Rafe did not press her for an answer. Though she was a witch woman, he had become so used to her peculiarities that he almost forgot what she was and the power of her magic. But it did occur to him that she never used her sorcery to bring game within killing distance of his weapons or to aid them in any similar way. When he asked her why she did not use her magic to that end, she answered him, "If you had a son would you walk for him?"

"No . . . He would have to do that on his own."

"Would you hunt for him?" she questioned.

"Only if he were ill, otherwise he would have to do it for himself."

"You must do it for yourself," Talum said. "I cannot do for you what you can do for yourself."

"But you need food and shelter too."

"And you have provided well for both needs," she answered.

No one could dispute what she said and he accepted it without comment. He was proud that he had kept the two of them from starving. Even Gumpa would not have been able to do more than he had done.

Now and then they passed close to other strongholds, but they always managed to quicken their pace and get away from them as quickly as possible. Then, when the ice left the river, they saw several ships moving toward the south.

Rafe had seen many such ships and knew that they were on their way to Miklagard to trade. But none of the vessels were nearly as large as those that had been attacked and burned by Gumpa at the bend in the river. He watched them as they went downstream.

"Pagar will get tribute from them," he said somewhat wistfully, "for their use of his portion of the river. . . . But he will never get from the traders what Gumpa got."

"I do not know of such things," the crone said with a shrug of her shoulders.

Rafe continued to speak about Gumpa, praising the man's skill as a hunter and saying that he might have been his adopted son if Enlil had not interfered.

Suddenly Talum stopped and put her finger to her

lips; then looking at him, she rolled her eyes to indicate there was something off to the left of them.

Rafe followed the movement of her eyes and saw a huge brown roebuck with eight points on its antlers. The animal, standing in a shaft of sunlight, was nibbling some young tender leaves off a low branch.

"I have not seen something like that since before the previous summer," he whispered.

The crone licked her lips. "Just the thought of tasting its meat," she told him, "makes my mouth water."

Motioning her not to move, Rafe dropped into a crouch. He worked his way toward the roebuck, making certain to remain downwind lest the animal get his scent and bolt. Should that happen, he would have to track him and hope he would have another chance to come upon him unawares. But the gods seldom offered a second chance if the first one was badly handled.

He crept forward, staying close to the ground. A bluejay landed on a branch of a nearby tree and clamorously scolded another jay.

Rafe stopped and only when he was sure that the roebuck was not disturbed by the noisy bird, did he risk moving again.

The animal suddenly stopped eating and lifted its head. It became tense: Something or someone else had disturbed it. . . . For several moments the roebuck did not move.

Rafe took a deep breath, leaped to his feet, and, rushing at the animal, he hurled his spear.

The roebuck bounded up and just as it started to run, Rafe's spear thudded into its side, splashing it red with blood. At the same moment an arrow caught the animal in the neck.

The roebuck fell sideways and struggled to regain its feet.

Rafe dashed toward the stricken prey, intending to

end its agony with a clean cut from his sword. Just as he reached the animal, another man came running at him.

"It is mine!" the man shouted, waving his sword in front of him. "It was my arrow that brought it down."

Rafe answered, "My spear landed true."

The man wore a leather helmet and clothes no different from those worn by other Rus.

"The kill is mine," the man shouted. "I was in the thicket there in front of him."

"And I was there," Rafe answered, pointing to where Talum was standing.

"The woman," the man said. "I will take her too." And he raised his sword challengingly.

"It is not worth dying for a crone—"

"Fool," the man shouted. "Blind fool . . . She is the most beautiful woman I have ever seen. . . . I will have her and the roebuck!"

Rafe halted the man's charge, meeting the slashing blow of the sword with his own weapon. Then he struck back, but the man withstood the attack. Back and forth they moved, each striking hard at the other and each defending himself against certain death.

The forest rang with the clang of metal against metal.

Sweat blinded the combatants but neither would dare risk the time it would have taken to clear his vision.

Rafe shouted, "We will share the roebuck. . . . There is more than enough for two."

The man grunted and continued to fight.

Rafe was filled with a growing weariness. He was finding it more and more difficult to leap away from the savage thrusts of his opponent.

"I will have your head on the point of my sword," the man growled.

Rafe realized that if he did not kill him soon, his

head would wind up on the point of the man's sword. Taking several deep breaths, he charged his would-be slayer with such ferocity that the man fell back from the attack and for a moment he lowered his sword. In that instant, Rafe plunged his own weapon into the man's chest.

The man dropped his sword and tried to pull the blade from his own body. But Rafe held it there until blood welled out of the man's mouth. Then he pulled the sword free, and the man fell.

With the back of his arm, Rafe wiped the sweat from his brow. He turned to where Talum was standing. . . . The crone had not moved. He nodded and went to the roebuck.

"Come," he called to Talum, "help me gut the animal."

"What will you do about the man you slew?" she asked.

"Leave him for the crows," Rafe answered. And then looking at her, he asked, "Did you hear what he said about you?"

She nodded.

"Did you bewitch him?" Rafe asked.

"No," Talum answered.

"How could he think you beautiful?"

"Every man sees what he wants to see," she answered.

Rafe glanced at the dead man, shook his head, and then gave himself up to the task of skinning the roebuck. . . .

XIII

Rafe took the meat he wanted from the roebuck and left the rest marked by a cairn on the bank of the river for other travelers. He placed the head of the roebuck nearby, on top of the mound of stones marking the grave of the man he slew.

"Whether it be Rus or Viking who comes to the store of meat," he told Talum, "he will know by the signs I leave that two men fought for the meat. . . . And knowing that one was killed for it, he will not waste it."

"It is the nature of men to waste whatever they obtain without effort," the crone answered peevishly.

Rafe looked up at the head of the roebuck and he said, "Crows will soon strip it down to the bone."

"And if we are not away from here soon," Talum cautioned, "the dead man's family and friends will not hesitate to strip us to the bone too."

Rafe agreed and though it was already night, they continued their journey until he was sure that they were not being followed. To further protect themselves, when they camped, it was not by the river, nor did they light a fire. As soon as the first light broke in the east, they were on the move again.

That afternoon, the forest began to thin and they passed close to a narrow place in the river where the roaring water churned white around huge black boulders. Two ships were being worked out of the water for portage around the rapids so that they would once again be able to travel north.

Rafe had never before seen this part of the river but he had heard about it from Gumpa, who had said it was one of the best places to attack the Viking ships.

Knowing that the Vikings would not hesitate to attack him and that he would not be able to defend himself against so many of them, Rafe prudently watched their efforts from behind some huge rocks. Only when all of them were aboard their ships and rowing north again, did he venture out of his hiding place.

Two days later they came upon another rapids deep in a chasm. It was even more fearsome than the previous one. Not only was there more white water, with even larger boulders, but also the roar of the swirling water was louder. Above it all hung a strange white mist that was full of the same colors that sometimes show in the sky after a rain.

Despite Talum's protestations, Rafe insisted on climbing down from the heights of the chasm to where the white water of the river rushed past the narrow bank.

She went part of the way with him. "I am not a goat," she shouted to him.

"Then stay where you are," Rafe called to her as he continued down. "I will be back shortly."

Talum sat down on a large flat rock and slowly shook her head.

The way to the bottom of the chasm was very steep. There were many places where a misstep would have plunged Rafe into the rushing water below. But he was surefooted enough to make the descent without imperiling his life.

Only when he reached the narrow rock ledge bordering the river and looked up to the heights did he realize he had used, for all its apparent difficulties, an artfully concealed trail which had been cut out of the chasm's rock face. He attributed it to the Vikings, who probably made use of it when portaging their ships. With a nod of approval, he silently expressed his admiration for them. He had never thought them to be more than ship handlers, though some were fighters as fierce as the Rus. . . .

Rafe gave his attention to the wild, surging water and the mist that rose above it. The water that rushed past the ledge on which he stood was almost black, while some distance from him, where the giant boulders were, it became a seething, twisting white fury.

He moved cautiously along the ledge to where the mist seemed to touch the walls of the chasm. The roar of the surging water overwhelmed the pounding of his own heart. He glanced up to the top of the chasm. The opening between the walls was so narrow he could scarcely see the thin strip of blue sky.

He stopped. The mist seemed to recede, curling back against the chasm's walls. Just as he was about to turn around and scramble back to the top of the chasm, he saw the unmistakable shape of a ship's hull caught between two enormous boulders, as if it were being held in the jaws of some dreaded river serpent. He strained to see more. . . . To come upon such a prize was indeed a rare occurrence: Gumpa had once done it and there was enough booty on the ship for everyone in the stronghold. . . .

Rafe scanned the water between him and the caught vessel. Along the side of the chasm it was less turbulent than anywhere else. He was a strong enough swimmer to reach a place close to the ship. But then he would have to make it through some terribly wild water before reaching the marooned vessel. The risk of him being taken by the river and smashed against the rocks was great. But the lure of what he might find aboard the ship was greater. He set his sword on the ledge and, taking only his knife, he dove into the icy water.

As he went down into the black depths, he was instantly seized by the intense cold. He fought to use his arms and legs, to free himself from the icy constriction that sought to stop his movements and kill him.

The current was far stronger than he had thought it would be. As if he were some sort of a child's toy, it turned him over and over. His lungs ached for air. Several times he was hurled against the submerged walls of the chasm. As he kicked himself away from them and struggled to break surface, his head was filled with a vision of Talum. He saw her seated on the rock, looking sadly down into the chasm where he was fighting for his life. . . .

"Your magic," he shouted up at her. And at that instant his head broke free of the water. His words echoed and re-echoed between the walls of the chasm.

Rafe gulped air and once more shouted up at Talum, "Your magic almost killed me." Again his words sounded over and over again.

More determined now than ever to reach the ship, he swam toward the swirling water that surrounded the stricken vessel. Over and over again the current pulled him down, forcing him to fight for his life. But slowly he succeeded in making his way to the ship.

Finally at the vessel's side, he wedged himself between two smashed oars and rested for several moments. When he was no longer breathing hard, he shouted, "I made it, Talum . . . I reached the ship!"

No sooner had the echo of his words faded than a woman called from above, "By the grace of Freyja you have come to save us!"

Rafe looked up and, peering over the side of the vessel, he saw a young woman with long blond hair.

Even in the misty dimness of the chasm, he could see her eyes were blue. Lifting himself between the splintered oars, he quickly gained the deck of the vessel.

His eyes swept the ship from stem to stern. Near the center, where the mast was, were three men. One was very old with gray hair and skin like old leather. Bending close to him and pointing to Rafe with his forefinger was a middle-aged man. There was some resemblance between him, the old man, and the young woman, especially around the mouth and nose. The third man stood slightly apart. He was Rafe's age, tall and powerfully built. He held a good sword in his hand. From the grim look on his face, he would not have needed much prodding to come rushing at Rafe, or anyone else who might unwittingly anger him.

"Where is the rest of the crew?" Rafe shouted above the sound of the rushing water.

"Taken by the river," the young woman answered.

The young man with the sword slowly made his way toward Rafe. "Who are you?" he yelled. Like the woman, he too had yellow hair. But his eyes were gray.

"Rafe . . . I am called Rafe."

The young man glanced back at the two older men.

"If he could swim here," the middle-aged one said, "then perhaps he might be able to swim back to the bank with a line around his waist. . . . He could save us if—"

"None of our men survived the river," the young man hastily countered. "How could he, unless he is not a man."

"I am as much a man as you," Rafe answered.

The young man suddenly leaped at him and drew his sword across Rafe's bare arm, leaving a line of blood. "At least he bleeds like a man," he said.

"Give me a sword," Rafe challenged, "and I will

show you I can also fight like a man, if that is the kind of sport you are after."

The middle-aged man quickly moved between them and, looking angrily at the man with the sword, he said, "Put up your sword, Lars, and give the man a chance to speak." Turning to Rafe, he asked how he came to be there.

"I saw your ship from the bank there," Rafe told him, pointing to where he had started. "I climbed down from the heights to get a closer look at the water and then the mist lifted and I saw this ship caught between the rocks."

"Ask him what he was doing on the heights," Lars demanded.

Rafe's eyes narrowed to slits, but controlling his anger, he answered, "I am going north with Talum. She is waiting for me on the heights."

The middle-aged man held out his hand. "My name is Garth. That is my father Ragnar and my daughter Thyri. Lars you know. We too are going north."

Suddenly amid the roar of the swirling water there was the terrible groaning of a ship being ground against the rocks; of a ship dying.

"Can you swim with a line around your waist?" Garth asked.

Rafe nodded.

"Our lives depend on you," he said, taking a thumb-thick line and securing it around Rafe's middle.

"I will do my best," Rafe answered, and without so much as a glance at Lars, he went over the side and dropped once more into the swirling water. . . .

The swim from the bank to the ship took all Rafe's strength, and for him to make the return journey with a line around his waist required superhuman strength. The instant he was in the water, he was sucked down into the depths by a fierce current that, like some giant serpent, wrapped its life-crushing coils around him.

Tumbling over and over, he fought to right himself. The line around his middle quickly became a huge web that sought to entrap him. But with powerful strokes and violent kicks, he was able to free himself of the line's danger and then, slashing through the swirling water, he broke surface where the river's flow was calmer, though much colder.

He gulped huge draughts of air into his starved lungs and looked back at the ship. He could still see it hanging between the gaping jaws of the rocks, and even more of it had been crushed.

Rafe turned toward the bank and started to swim toward it. The cold numbed his body, making his teeth chatter. But he never paused, lest he give in to the desire to stop, to close his eyes and let the river claim him.

Finally he was there: at the place from which he had started. He lifted his right hand to take hold of the rock. Though his fingers brushed against it, he lacked the strength to gain a firm grip.

He shook his head and tried again. He failed. He used his left hand instead of his right. He could hold nothing with either one.

He felt himself being taken by the river and clawed his way along the rocky bank. The skin on his blood-covered hands was torn. In desperation, he hurled himself up on the bank. Half of him was free of the river and half of him was still held in its murderous grasp.

With agonizing slowness, Rafe pulled himself bit by bit higher onto the bank. To force the river to yield the rest of his body was slow, painful work.

Exhausted by the struggle to bring the line from the ship to the bank, he lay very still. His body ached with weariness, but as soon as he began to feel some heat in his limbs again he crawled to where he could secure the line. Removing it from his waist, he lashed it to an upright piece of rock. Giving it several strong tugs to let Garth and the others aboard the vessel know he had succeeded, he sat down and waited for them to make their way to the safety of the bank.

Except for having spoken about Talum to Garth, Rafe had been too occupied to give her much thought. But now as he waited to be joined by the others from the ship, he looked up to the top of the chasm and wondered how she was faring without him. Though she was a crone and only the gods knew the power of her magic, he felt oddly responsible for her. They had already traveled a long way together and no doubt still had a long way to go before they reached the north. But once he reached it, he had no idea what he would do there either with himself or with her.

Suddenly, he was diverted from his thoughts by shouting that came from the ship. Though there were already long gray shadows in the chasm, he could see that the old man, Ragnar, was already over the side of the vessel and struggling hand over hand on the rope to make his way to the bank.

Below the struggling old man the swirling waters leaped up and tried to tug him down.

"Keep going," Garth shouted above the roar of the water. "Keep going!"

"It is too much for me," Ragnar yelled.

Thyri pleaded with her grandfather not to stop.

Rafe scrambled to his feet and, going to the edge of the bank, he called out to Ragnar, "Fight the water . . . Kick it away from you. . . ."

"I lack the strength . . . I lack the strength," the old man answered.

As Rafe heard the words, he felt another presence close by, and looking back toward the rock face of the chasm, he saw Death.

"For the old man?" he shouted.

But Death would not answer.

A moment later there was a forlorn cry.

Rafe looked to where Ragnar was. The line was empty!

Another cry sounded but this one came from the ship and Garth went over the side into the swirling water to save his father.

Again Rafe turned to Death, but he was already walking slowly up the steep rocky path and behind him were the spirits of Ragnar and Garth. . . . Garth's spirit turned to Rafe and in a low moan that breached the world of the dead, he cried out for his daughter; then he, Ragnar, and Death vanished.

Rafe looked toward the ship. Thyri was already halfway across and Lars, anxious to be off of the dying ship, was on the line too, working his way toward the safety of the bank.

As soon as Thyri was close enough Rafe went once more into the icy water and carried her on his back to the river bank. He offered the same service to Lars, who scornfully refused it, shouting that he was man enough to reach the bank on his own. And so he was. . . .

Almost as soon as Lars was safe, what was left of the ship broke up with a tortured screeching and thunderous cracking of timber. Lars stood and watched the ship's final agony, while Thyri sat off to one side and silently grieved for her father and grandfather.

When nothing of the vessel could be seen or heard, Lars faced Rafe and said, "It was a good ship and it served us well." He looked toward Thyri and shook his head. "All that she owned was on the ship . . . All that—" He could no longer speak and uttered a weary sigh.

Night came swiftly, and high above the narrow

opening at the top of the chasm a band of star-filled sky could be seen.

"Tomorrow, at first light," Rafe said as they huddled around a small fire of driftwood, "we will climb to the top and after I get Talum, the four of us can go north."

"Why are you going north?" Lars questioned. "You are obviously a Rus. . . . Your home is here."

"I have no home," Rafe answered.

For a while none of them spoke and Rafe was able to see, even in the play of firelight, how very beautiful Thyri was. She was far more beautiful than Astrid. Her skin was white and her lips full and red, like wild cherries. Under her tunic he could see the outline of her full breasts and, when she stood, the lovely swell of her hips.

Having taken his fill of her with his eyes, he turned toward Lars and in a respectful voice he asked how the ship managed to become wedged between the two black rocks.

"The mist," Lars answered after a few moments of hesitation, "the mist which was white and full of the colors of the rainbow suddenly turned black. We did not even know we had run aground until the rocks loomed up over us."

"And the crew," Rafe questioned, "what happened to them?"

"Many were flung over the side by the sudden backlash of their oars," Lars told him. "Others were carried away by the sudden torrent that poured over the ship. The rest, seeing the hopelessness of the situation, went over the side and tried to swim to safety. . . . We saw the river take all of them."

Thyri began to weep softly.

"Now tell me the truth," Lars said. "How did you manage to swim out to the ship?"

"I already told you," Rafe replied.

"I am not a fool," Lars told him. "I know from my experiences in Miklagard that there are men who are not men but look like men so that they cannot be called anything else."

"I am a man," Rafe said, looking at Thyri. "No more or less than that."

"We will see," Lars answered.

Rafe did not answer and, stretching out close to the fire, he was swiftly taken by sleep. . . .

Before dawn came, Rafe was awake. Lars was still asleep but Thyri was standing at the edge of the river.

Rafe went to her and said he was sorry that she had lost her father and grandfather.

"Thank you for all you have done for us," she said. "I did not expect to live to see another morning."

"I am sure you and yours would have done as much for me," he answered courteously.

"My father was a very brave man and in his day so was my grandfather."

Rafe nodded and said, "You yourself are no less brave."

"If I am brave," she told him, "it is out of fear. . . . But Ragnar and Garth were brave without regard for fear. . . . My father was renowned among his own people and also among those of Miklagard."

"Lars will see you safely to the rest of your family," Rafe said.

"I do not know what Lars will do," she said, "now that my dowry is gone. . . . I do not know what he will do."

Rafe fought down the desire to sweep her into his arms and comfort her. "It is time to go," he told her gently. "I will wake Lars. The climb will be hard."

"No harder than anything else has been these past

two days," she answered with a stifled sob. "No harder than anything else . . ."

Rafe woke Lars. With Thyri between them, they started up the steep trail that led to the top of the chasm.

XIV

The climb out of the chasm was arduous. Several times each of them lost their footing but, luckily, each time they managed to regain it before a disaster could occur. When they reached the top, they were winded and wet with sweat.

"Rest here," Rafe told his companions, "while I find Talum."

"I will go with you," Lars said.

"If that is your pleasure," Rafe answered with a shrug, "then come along." And he started off to find the crone. But there was no sign of her, either at the flat rock, where he had left her, or in the vicinity. He called to her but there was no answer.

"Enough of your game!" Lars suddenly shouted.

Rafe looked questioningly at him. Then in a quiet voice, he said, "I told you true . . . I left her there on the flat rock."

Lars snorted with disdain.

"Believe what you want," Rafe said, and returning to where they had left Thyri, he threw himself down on the ground to rest.

"There never was an old woman," Lars told Thyri, who was still standing. He pointed to Rafe, and explained, "I do not believe anything else he has said either: No man just climbs down in the chasm and swims out to a ship in such fierce white water."

"You are a fool!" Rafe exclaimed.

Flushed with anger, Lars growled, "No man calls me a fool." And he raised his sword challengingly toward Rafe. "No Rus ever risked his life for a Viking, unless there was some trick behind it."

"I have no wish to fight," Rafe said. "Put up your sword and talk about—"

"There is nothing to talk about," Lars responded. "I will take Thyri with me."

"Go then," Rafe told him. "I will follow. But first I want to find Talum."

"There is the matter of who and what you are that must be settled before I do anything else."

Rafe looked toward Thyri and said, "Lead him away from here."

Lars waved his sword and demanded that Rafe take up his weapon. "Doing this now," Lars commented, "will save me from having to do it later."

"Please, Lars," Thyri implored, "do him no harm. . . . He has saved our lives and—"

"Silence!" he shouted. "I will not have a woman tell me what to do. I will do what suits me, what pleases me."

"You would not speak to me this way if my father were here," she shouted at him. "You would be more than willing to do whatever I asked."

"Silence!" he roared, and going to her, he struck her hard across the mouth. "You have nothing to give me but your poor miserable self and hopefully I will be able to get a good price for you from someone along the way. . . . I want no wife without a dowry and as for a thrall, I would rather sell you with your maidenhead intact. Virgins always fetch better prices than those women who have already been used." Then turning to Rafe, he said, "I saw the way you have been looking at her. . . . I cannot let you interfere with my plans."

Rafe scrambled to his feet and drew his sword.

"So now you will fight, eh?" Lars laughed.

The two men circled one another. Dust swirled around their legs.

Lars shouted epithets at his opponent.

Rafe's face was expressionless. He said nothing.

"Stand and fight," Lars said. "That is, if you can stand and fight!" He made a sudden slashing movement at Rafe that caught him on his right arm and drew blood.

Rafe jumped back.

Their blades suddenly clanged together. The blow made the swords tremble in their hands.

Breathing hard and wet with sweat, they circled one another again.

Lars struck again, this time running his blade across Rafe's left shoulder. "You are a better swimmer than you are a swordsman," he shouted exuberantly.

Once more their blades met in a dreadful clang, staggering each one of them.

Rafe was the first to recover and, bounding forward, he drove his sword into Lars' stomach, picked him up on the blade, and flung him against a boulder.

Lars screamed when the blade plunged into his vitals, and flailed the air with his legs and arms when he was lifted above Rafe's head, but by the time he struck the rock he was silent.

"Fool," Rafe screamed at the dead man. "Fool!" Weak from his own wounds, he took a handful of grass and wiped the blood from his sword. Then he staggered to where Thyri cowered and said, "I did not want his blood on my hands."

"He would have gladly had yours on his hands," she answered, helping him to sit down.

Rafe slept most of the day away. By late afternoon, he said, "I think it would be better if we did not spend the night here."

Thyri agreed and, lending her body to support him,

they slowly continued to follow the river north, though the water was far below them in the rocky chasm. That night Rafe managed to snare a rabbit and Thyri cooked it. The meat and the marrow from the bones gave him strength.

But Rafe slept badly. He was unable to stop thinking about Talum and wondered if she had been taken captive by some other people. Disturbed by the possibility she might be in danger, he sat up. As he thought, he stirred the embers until he coaxed new flames from them and placed a few more pieces of wood in the fire.

"What do you see in the fire?" Thyri asked in a low voice.

Rafe turned to her. She was sitting close to his right side. He had been so deep in thought about Talum that he had not heard Thyri move.

She asked him again what he saw in the flames.

"Nothing," he answered. "But if I could, I would try to see what happened to Talum."

"I have heard it said that if a person stares long and hard at them they can see the dead."

"Yes, I have heard that too," Rafe said without conviction.

"I would like to see my father and grandfather," she told him with a soft sob.

He nodded and though he did not say anything, he wondered if by staring into the flames he might sometime be able to see his mother.

"Will you sell me, Rafe?" Thyri asked in a hesitant voice.

"No."

She moved closer to him.

Rafe felt the softness of her breast against his arm. He looked at her.

"It is all I have to give," she said.

Aroused, Rafe put his arms around her. He drew

her down to the ground. His lips found hers. Their kiss was long and passionate. Their tongues met. Rafe undid the ties of her tunic. His hands moved over her bare breasts and down her flat stomach.

"In Miklagard a woman is taught to give a man pleasure without taking his man-thing into her slit," she whispered.

"But how—"

She laughed softly. Pulling away, she told him to remove his clothes, while she did the same. When the two of them were naked, she directed him to lie flat on his back. She put her lips to his and at the same time reached down to caress his man-thing.

Rafe slid his hands over her naked breasts and around her back but Thyri began slowly to move down the length of his body. As she did, she used her lips and tongue on the nipples of his breasts, then in the swirl of his navel, and finally, giving him exquisite delight, the tip of her tongue flicked across the head of his man-thing.

He arched his body toward her, hoping to place more of his man-thing in the warm cavern of her mouth.

But she pulled away, saying, "There is more pleasure in the waiting."

"I will wait another time," he said urgently. "Now I want you." And reaching down, he pulled her up to him.

Willingly she opened her naked thighs for him.

His hand found her sex and gently taking hold of its lips, he caressed it.

Thyri moaned with pleasure.

And he placed her under him.

"Be gentle," she said in a low voice.

Rafe went into her.

She cried out in pain. Then as he went deeper into her body, she clutched at him with intense ecstasy.

Together they began to move.

She tightened her hold on him and wrapped her legs around his bare back. "Oh it is so good," she purred. "So good!"

"Yes," he gasped.

Their pace quickened and soon Thyri was crying out her delight and Rafe made low throaty sounds of pleasure. They came to the moment of shuddering ecstasy together.

Rafe buried his face between the two mounds of her lovely breasts, while she heaved herself up against him and raked his back with her fingers. . . .

Later when they could speak again, Thyri said, "I have much to teach you that I was taught in Miklagard."

"And I will learn all of it," Rafe answered, fondling her bare breasts. "All of it."

They spoke to each other in low tones, almost as if they were afraid to be overheard.

Thyri said, "I hope my father and grandfather are with Odin in Valhalla and not in Hel."

Rafe told her, "The gods pick the very best for their own and from what you have told me about your father and grandfather, they must be numbered among them." And then he asked her more about Lars.

"He sailed with my father for several years," she said. "And in time he became second in command to my father and then he asked for me."

"Did you have feelings for him?"

"Not enough to let him possess me, as you have," she answered. "Sometimes I thought he cheated my father but I had nothing for proof."

"And in the north," Rafe questioned, "where is your home?"

"At the stronghold of Vikar, jarl of the island."

"Do you know where the island is, or its name?"

"Zurd, a half-day's sail to the west from the place where the river and the sea meet."

"That is where we will go," Rafe said with determination.

"Is it where you wanted to go?"

"I was just going north," he answered.

She laughed softly and told him it was foolish for him to think of doing something like that. "The country is cold and hard and the men are even harder than the country."

Rafe shrugged. He did not know what to answer.

"Now it is your turn to tell me about yourself," Thyri said, propping herself up on an elbow. "Tell me about you."

He told her little more than he had already.

"But I want to know where you come from!" she exclaimed.

"I do not know. I was taken captive when I was only a small boy . . . several months old."

Thyri reached out and gently caressed his chest. With a yawn, she said, "Vikar is my uncle. He is an old man . . . but he will treat us gently, very gently." The next moment, she was asleep. . . .

Rafe slept wrapped in Thyri's embrace. He had not had a woman for some time and the pleasure Thyri had given him had far surpassed anything he had previously experienced. That she knew the ways of Miklagard to please a man gave her an aura of excitement that had been absent from his encounters with other women.

Even in sleep her nearness aroused him and, pressing closer to her, he found himself in a delicious state of intoxication with what he possessed. But in his slumber he was disturbed by the melancholy sound of a woman weeping. . . . It eventually roused him

107

and he listened carefully to Thyri. But she was in a deep sleep.

The sound he heard was coming from somewhere else. He thought it might be Talum, wandering around lost. He called softly to her.

There was no response.

He called again; this time louder.

Thyri awakened with a start and asked, "What is wrong?"

"I think Talum might be out there," he answered, then shouted for Talum.

"She does not answer," Thyri said.

"I heard a woman weeping," Rafe explained.

"Perhaps it was only a night bird," she suggested.

"I know the difference between a bird's call and the sound of a woman weeping," he said, taking hold of his sword and scrambling to his feet.

"It could be anything," she told him, grabbing hold of his hand. "The night is full of evil spirits. . . . Some in the form of a woman entice men to lie with them and they they suck his blood. Others in the body of a man do the same to women. . . . Stay here with me."

"I will go no farther than the birches over there," he said. "But if Talum is nearby, I want to find her."

"Why is she so important? She is nothing to you."

"I must find her," he said, pulling away from Thyri's hold. "I will feel much better about everything when she is with us."

"I will go with you," she offered.

"No . . . Stay here . . . I will not be gone long," Rafe told her, and he moved quickly away from their small campsite. There was a crescent moon and, though yellow, it kept much of its light to itself.

His search yielded nothing and Rafe returned to Thyri. He stretched out next to her and she pressed close to him.

Their passions were quickly aroused and, this time, he did not wait to learn anything else from Thyri. Giving way to his own need, he took her powerfully. By the violence of his actions he also gave her enormous pleasure.

Sleep came swiftly but once more it brought to Rafe the sound of a woman weeping. . . . And then he saw the same desolate rock-strewn place he had seen once before in a dream. And in the shadow of a huge boulder a woman sat weeping.

"He is lost to you," a man told the woman.

Rafe could not see the man who spoke but his voice was familiar.

"She has him now," the man said.

The woman only sobbed. . . .

Rafe opened his eyes. The moon was down and the dark sky was filled with stars. The memory of his dream vanished and though he tried hard to remember what he had dreamt, he could not.

He searched the sky for the star that guides men at night to the north. He found it and nodded with satisfaction. But he did not sleep and when the first light came into the eastern sky, he wondered why the night had passed so quickly.

Suddenly he heard his name. He opened his eyes and saw Thyri bending over him. Her bare breasts were just above his face. He drew her down to him and put his lips to the nipple of one breast and then the other.

She sighed with delight.

"I want you again," he told her passionately, pushing the bottom of her tunic high above her thighs.

"Oh, yes!" she exclaimed. Just as she was about to let him slide over her, she glanced up toward the birches and screamed!

Within moments several mounted men galloped clear of the trees and came rushing toward them.

Rafe scrambled to his feet. He tried to lift his sword but an arrow swooshed through the air and came between him and his weapon.

The riders brought their mounts to an instant halt. The men were from the east. They were fierce fighters. They rode smaller horses than the Rus but they spoke a similar tongue.

One of them, more powerfully built than the others, eased his horse slightly forward and pointing at Thyri's bare breasts nodded and said he would have her first.

Wide-eyed with fear, she moved backward.

The man laughed.

The other horsemen also laughed.

"Tie him up," the man ordered, pointing to Rafe.

Two men dismounted. They slipped a rope over their captive's head and around his neck. Then they bound his hands behind him.

"Now to the woman!" the leader exclaimed. He dismounted and, going to Thyri, he tore the tunic from her body with one swift downward motion of his hand.

She screamed and tried to fight him off.

He tossed her to the ground. Slapping her across the face to make her more docile, he pried open her naked thighs and jammed his man-thing into her body.

She shouted for Rafe.

He stood and watched her being raped.

The man grabbed hold of her flailing arms and, laughing, he pinned her to the ground. Then as he began to move, she became less and less violent. Soon she was moaning with pleasure, and thrashing her head from side to side. "See how Baugi rides this one," he called to his followers.

The other horsemen shouted encouragement to him.

Spellbound, Rafe watched Thyri's resistance change to acceptance and then to delight.

Baugi brought her to a shuddering climax as he

himself grunted his pleasure. Then getting up, he pointed to one of the other men and said, "There, she is ready now. . . . I have broken her for you."

One by one the men took their pleasure with Thyri and with each of them she was passionate. When it was over, she was allowed to wrap her nakedness in the remnants of her tunic, before she too was tethered by the neck and her hands bound.

"I will keep her for myself," Baugi said. "But the man I will sell into slavery, though from the look of him he will not make a good slave." Then he ordered his men to mount up and, with the ends of the ropes that bound Rafe and Thyri around their necks, he moved his horse at a walk.

Thyri began to sob.

When twilight came and they made camp for the night, Rafe was thrown a piece of meat and given water before he was staked down. Thyri was taken by Baugi to be used for his pleasure.

Rafe waited until everyone was alseep before he attempted to work his hands free, but they were too tightly bound for him to do anything. After a while, he slept too.

For several days they continued to travel, sometimes close to the river, other times to the east of it, but always they moved north.

Though Baugi took his pleasure with Thyri at night, she was treated no better than Rafe during the day. She tried to speak to him but he would not answer her.

One day when morning had not yet passed and the sky was an intense blue, Baugi halted his men and, pointing off to the east, he said, "Below that cloud of yellow dust is a caravan." And looking back at Rafe, he told him he would soon be sold.

"And what am I to say to that?" Rafe asked.

"So you can speak when you want to," Baugi re-

sponded, jerking so hard on the line that he brought
Rafe to his knees. Then handing the line that tethered
Thyri to one of his men, he rode toward the caravan
with Rafe trailing behind him.

Long before he reached the line of horses and asses,
Baugi shouted, "I come in peace; I come to sell a
slave. . . . I come in peace; I come to sell a slave."

The leader of the caravan was a tall, thin, red-
bearded man with bright green eyes. He raised his
right hand to signal his men to stop and turned his
mount toward Baugi.

"I captured this man and his woman a few days
ago," Baugi said. "The woman I will keep, but for a
good horse or a few pieces of gold you can have the
man."

The red-bearded man nodded solemnly, while his
green eyes flicked back and forth between Baugi and
Rafe. Then he asked, "Where are the rest of your men?"

Baugi gestured behind him. But he nervously took
up the slack in the line that held Rafe. "He will make
a good thrall," he said, easing his mount backward.

"Then leave him," the red-bearded man replied in
an even tone. "Leave him and be happy your gift to
us has enabled you to escape with your life." As he
finished speaking several of the horsemen left the line
and began to form a circle around Baugi.

He was about to object, but seeing the riders were
fast closing in on him, he dropped the end of Rafe's
tether and, spurring his horse, he galloped away.

The red-bearded man laughed until he complained
his sides hurt. Then to Rafe he said, "It is much easier
for one thief to steal from another than from an honest
man. . . ."

XV

"And what of the woman?" the red-bearded man asked, squinting down at Rafe from the back of a magnificent black stallion.

Rafe shrugged. He did not know how to answer. He no longer had any feelings for Thyri, at least not any tender ones. She had betrayed him with her wantonness. A woman with such hot blood would deceive her husband. She would make a fool of him in the eyes of other men.

"Well, speak up!" the man exclaimed impatiently. "Some men would rather be rid of their women, while others prefer to hold what they have and not run the risk of having to learn something new."

"I want her," Rafe answered, knowing that if he left Thyri with Baugi, he would soon tire of her and then she would be sold to anyone with enough gold to meet his price.

"That took some thinking on your part," the bearded man laughed. Then with a quick gesture and a sharp command, he dispatched six riders to follow Baugi. "Bring back the woman. And do not molest her on the way to us. . . . We will continue riding north." Then beckoning Rafe closer to him, he leaned down and cut the rope from his neck. "Can you ride?" he asked, straightening up.

"As well, if not better than you can," Rafe answered, looking up into his gray eyes.

"Bring him a horse," the red-bearded man ordered. Then he asked, "How are you called?"

"Rafe."

"I am known as Red Beard. . . . The second to me is Garith," he said, pointing to the man behind him. "The others you might in time get to know."

Garith was a compactly built man with a barrel-like chest, big hands, and a heavy-boned face with black brooding eyes and black hair.

From the rear of the column, one of the men led a large brown horse. It was every bit as big as the animal Red Beard rode. As it came closer, Rafe could see the wild look in its bloodshot eyes.

"If you ride as well as you say you do," Red Beard told him, "you should be able to ride him. . . . If you are thrown, I will kill you, or I will let him pound you to death with his hoofs."

Rafe was about to object.

"It is our way," Red Beard said nonchalantly. "We must have some way of judging what kind of man you are."

Sometime in the past, Rafe remembered having been told by Gumpa that besides the Rus, who lived in strongholds along the river, and the Vikings, who used the river on their journey to and from Miklagard, there was another group of people who also lived along the river and were good horsemen. Gumpa had called them Khazars. He had said that according to their own stories they had come from a land far to the south, a place even beyond Miklagard.

"Mount!" Red Beard ordered, beginning to draw his sword.

Rafe nodded and went to the animal. "Easy," he whispered. "Easy there." And calling to Red Beard, he asked if the horse had a name.

"No. But he is known as a killer of men," he answered with a laugh.

The horse snorted nervously. With his bloodshot eyes, he looked balefully at the man in front of him.

Rafe whispered soothingly, "My horse Agni was your color. . . . He was not as big as you are but he was swift and had good staying power."

The horse suddenly threw up its head and neighed loudly.

"Whatever you are telling him," Red Beard called out, "he does not seem to like. Promise him a mare and perhaps he will take more kindly to you."

Rafe ignored the gibe and gave his full attention to the animal. "Neither one of us wants this," he said in a soft voice. "But it must be done." As he spoke, he moved to the left side of the horse. He stroked its flanks.

The animal looked back at him. None of the wild rage that had previously been in his eyes had gone; if anything, he looked even angrier. Without warning, the animal suddenly whirled toward Rafe and tried to bite him.

The sudden movement knocked Rafe to the ground.

The horse reared up and, flailing its forelegs, came crashing down.

Rafe rolled away just as the great hoofs slammed against the ground, where he had been.

The horse neighed angrily. With a wild shaking of its huge head, it pawed the ground.

Rafe sprang to his feet. He ran straight toward the animal and at the last moment, when it was ready to make its charge, he darted off to the side. A moment later he leaped into the saddle.

The horse reared, neighed loudly and, twisting its head around, tried to bite the man on its back.

Rafe flung his foot out and struck him in the nose with such force that the animal neighed in pain.

The men in the column called out to the horse, urging him to throw the rider to the ground.

Once more the beast reared up, clawing at the air with his front legs.

Rafe held fast.

The horse suddenly began to gallop and then came to a halt.

The sudden stop almost sent Rafe over the top of the animal's head. But he held his body to the saddle.

The horse dropped to the ground and tried to roll over its rider.

Rafe leaped clear. But as soon as the beast got to its feet, he was back in the saddle.

Over and over again the horse made every effort to rid himself of the rider, but no matter what he did the man on his back remained there. Even when he began to buck, his rider stayed with him.

Soon the animal's flanks were lathered and he was foaming at the mouth. His efforts to throw Rafe diminished.

Rafe used the reins, making the animal feel the bit in his mouth. Whenever the horse wanted to go one way, he roughly jerked its head in the opposite direction. He brought it to a stop at his will and moved it into a walk then a trot and finally, into a gallop.

When he was sure that he had broken the animal, Rafe rode up to Red Beard and said in a loud voice, "He will kill no more men."

There was the sparkle of laughter in Red Beard's eyes and, with a nod, he said, "He is yours. What will you call him?"

Rafe patted the animal's wet flanks. "Yggr," he answered.

"I thought you were a Rus," Red Beard commented.

Rafe nodded.

"Now," Red Beard told him, "we must continue." And he gave the order for the column to move. "Come, ride alongside of me, Rafe."

"Am I to be your thrall?" Rafe asked him.

"We have no slaves," Red Beard answered. "It is not our way to keep others in bondage."

Rafe did not ask any more questions. After a while he dropped back and rode alongside of Garith, who said nothing but from time to time gave him dark looks. But Rafe pretended not to notice them. . . .

By late afternoon, Red Beard swung the column toward the river. A short while afterward, a cloud of yellow dust appeared.

"That will be my men," Red Beard said, looking back over his shoulder at Rafe. "We will soon see if they have your woman with them."

Rafe touched his heels to Yggr's flanks. The animal responded instantly. A few moments later he was alongside of Red Beard.

The cloud of yellow dust moved rapidly toward them; then it slowed, stopped altogether, and began to settle. Gradually the cloud thinned and out of its depths several dark figures emerged.

Rafe was still too far away to see if Thyri was with them.

"If you wish, you may ride ahead," Red Beard said.

Rafe shook his head and thanked him for his offer. "I can be patient a little while longer," he explained.

Red Beard shrugged but did not comment.

The figures in the distance became more sharply defined. Red Beard had sent out six riders and now there were seven. They had returned with Thyri or they had taken a captive.

"You are indeed a patient man," Red Beard said, looking archly at Rafe. "If she were my woman, I know I would not ride so slowly toward her."

"I have been taught how to be patient," he answered.

"Passion is not usually kindred to patience," the Khazar chieftain said. "More often than not passion

117

overwhelms patience, at least that has been my experience."

Rafe remained silent.

Suddenly a woman's voice called out to Rafe. An instant later, a thin swirl of dust rose above the distant figures and a lone rider galloped toward them.

"She is less patient than you," Red Beard laughed.

Rafe was too embarrassed to remain there and, with a shout, he sent Yggr into a gallop. Very soon he was within sight of Thyri and slowed to a trot.

She too slowed her mount.

They came together at a walk. As they reined to a halt, side by side, Thyri flung her arms around him. "I thought I would never see you again," she sobbed.

Her nearness stirred him. Embracing her, he told her, "I could not leave you with Baugi . . . I could not abandon you to him and to what would come after him."

"Baugi and one of the other men fled," she said. "The rest were killed by those who brought me to you."

"Khazars," Rafe responded. "That is what they are. . . ." And taking the reins from her hands, he led her mount back to meet the column.

"You should have told me that your woman was so comely," Red Beard said, after Rafe presented Thyri to him, "and I would have rushed to meet her myself."

Thyri reddened and thanked him for his kind words.

When Rafe led Thyri back to Garith, he acknowledged her with a silent nod and once again looked so blackly at Rafe that she was eager to be away from him. And when they dropped back behind Garith, she asked Rafe what was wrong between them.

"I do not know," Rafe answered. "But whatever it is, I am sure it can be settled without difficulty."

For a while they rode without speaking. But then Thyri said, "I know you are wroth with me for—"

"It is not something to speak about," he told her.

She turned her face away, but at the same time she said, "I could not help myself. . . . Do you understand that?" She looked at him again, waiting for an answer.

With a weary sigh, he nodded.

"I would not willingly lie with another man," Thyri said.

"Yes, I know that," he responded. And after a pause he added, "It is best left behind us."

"You have my word I will give you more pleasure than you ever dreamed possible."

He reached across the narrow space that separated them and, touching her hand, he said, "We will give each other pleasure."

"Yes," Thyri answered. "Oh, yes!" There were tears in her eyes and she used the back of her hand to wipe them away. "Twice you saved my life. I will never forget that."

"I do not want your gratitude," Rafe said. "No man who calls himself a man would have done less."

Thyri took hold of his hand and put it to her lips. "We will have each other," she exclaimed in a low, throaty voice, "tonight we will have each other!"

The column continued to ride north along the river until the sun was low in the west and the sky was streaked with fire; then Red Beard gave the order to halt for the night and make camp.

Immediately guards were set out around the edge of the encampment. Only after Red Beard was absolutely certain the guards were well placed did he permit cooking fires to be lighted.

Rafe and Thyri were invited to join Red Beard at his fire and share his food. As they ate, he asked them how they came to be captives of someone like Baugi.

"He and his men came upon us in the morning," Thyri answered. "Our heads were too full of sleep to—"

"And no doubt your bodies were too weak from a night of pleasure," he said laughingly.

Rafe moved uneasily.

"It is all right," Red Beard commented, moving his gray eyes to him. "I am that way too when I am with my women." Then handing Rafe a skin bag, he said, "It is wine. . . . Drink and we will speak of other matters."

The wine was sweet and good. Rafe handed the skin to Thyri, looking first to Red Beard for permission. He nodded and said, "Wine is as good for a woman as it is for a man."

After the wineskin was back in Red Beard's possession, he reached into another bag for a pipe and tobacco. Gumpa smoked sometimes and some other Rus, Rafe had seen, smoked also, but with something called a water pipe.

"Can you fight as well as you ride?" Red Beard asked.

"Oh, I have seen him wield a sword," Thyri told him excitedly. "And he is a powerful fighter."

Red Beard made a clicking sound with his tongue. "Are you also as good with a spear and a bow?" he asked.

"The people in the stronghold said I was as good as Gumpa and he was our chieftain."

"And where is your stronghold?" Red Beard questioned.

"South on the river."

"How many days south on the river?" he asked, stirring the embers of the fire and putting more faggots on it.

Rafe thought for several moments before answering. He knew all too well that Red Beard and those with him were marauders, that like Baugi and his men they lived by plunder.

"Would you say two days, three days, or more?"

"Much more," Rafe said. "When I left the snows were still falling and it was bitter cold."

Red Beard accepted the explanation with a silent nod. For a while he busied himself cutting meat. Then, bowing his head, he spoke many words in a strange language.

Rafe looked around to see if one of his men might be close by but there was no one. The nearest was Garith and he was several paces away.

"I was giving thanks to Jhavh," Red Beard explained, "for the food he put before us."

"Odin?" Rafe questioned, thinking that other people might call the god by a different name.

Red Beard laughed and shook his head.

"Thor?" Rafe questioned, knowing that among some people he is favored over Odin.

Again Red Beard shook his head, but this time he said, "There is only one God, the God that went before the Israelites when Moses led them out of the land of Egypt."

"I have heard, even in Miklagard, that some people worship the Son of God and he is called Christ."

Red Beard guffawed and called to Garith. "These two talk of gods as if they were as numerous as apples on a tree," he said.

"They are no more than savages; they know nothing about Jhavh," Garith answered.

"The old gods," Red Beard said solemnly, "are false gods. . . . They are demons and the one who claimed to be the Son of God, I was told, died on a cross for his boasting."

"But there are men who call themselves Christ-priests," Thyri responded. "They teach what He taught."

121

"So I have also heard," Red Beard said. "But to believe what they say a man might as well believe that the moon is the sun and the sun is the moon."

"I will put my trust in Odin," Rafe commented resolutely.

"It is not our way to seek converts," Red Beard said.

"But from all the gods to choose, how did your people come to yours?" Thyri questioned.

"He chose us. . . . There is a covenant between my people and Him," Red Beard answered.

"And does it hold good on the river and north to where the Vikings live?"

"It holds good wherever we are and forever."

"I will stay with Odin!" Rafe said.

Red Beard nodded and casually asked, "Will you also stay with us?"

Rafe glanced at Thyri. But there was nothing in the expression on her face or in her eyes to tell him what her thoughts on the matter might be. "I am going north," Rafe said.

"But why not south, or east or west?"

"Thyri's uncle is a jarl and I gave my word I would take her to him."

Red Beard said, "A man who gives his word must honor it. Of course," he added, "if you honor it somewhat later than sooner, you would still be honoring it."

"I go north also," Rafe said, "to find my destiny." He did not expect the words. He was as surprised by what he said as Red Beard and Thyri were to hear it. Yet strangely enough, he meant every word.

Altogether unsure of what the Rus was talking about, Red Beard stirred the embers again before he responded. "I would deprive no man of his destiny," he told Rafe, "as long as he does not deprive me of mine. —Wait, hear me out before you speak. There are two points to consider: the first has to do with your destiny. Suppose it was your destiny to go no farther north than you have already come. Then suppose it was my destiny to meet with you. With our separate destinies coming together that way, it would seem that in some way they were meant to combine."

"That could be so," Rafe agreed.

"Yes, that was what I was thinking when you spoke of destiny," Red Beard told him. "Since you were delivered into my hands and I will not make a slave of either you or your woman, could it be that destiny meant you to stay with me and my men for a while?"

Rafe nodded.

"Then you agree to remain with us?" Red Beard asked enthusiastically.

"For what purpose?"

Red Beard smiled; his gray eyes sparkled with fire. "For a good purpose," he said, "I assure you . . . And since you will be with us, you will have an equal share of the booty that comes our way. After all, if you share in the danger, you are entitled to share in the—"

"And if I refuse?" Rafe questioned.

The smile left Red Beard's face and the sparkle left his eyes. "Ingratitude," he said, "causes much of the trouble between men, to say nothing of the trouble between men and women. . . . But should you show such ingratitude, I would have to kill you and either take your woman for my concubine or give her to one of my men."

"I do not have a choice then, do I?"

"Oh, yes . . . Between life and death, which is to my way of thinking the only true choice a man or woman ever has."

"I will stay," Rafe said. "But no longer than it takes me to fulfill your purpose."

"You have my word on that," Red Beard said. "Another drink of wine before you and your woman go to sleep?"

Rafe drank from the skin bag and so did Thyri.

"I already no longer remember the time when you were not with us," Red Beard said.

Rafe looked at him impassively.

"It is my way of extending a welcome to you," Red Beard explained.

"Thank you," Thyri answered.

Red Beard looked up at the sky. A quarter moon had risen above the tops of the trees. "We have a long ride tomorrow and for several days afterward," he said, stretching his hands high over his head. Then calling to one of his men, he provided Rafe and Thyri with blankets. "I know you are not used to such things," he said to Rafe.

"Oh, I am," Thyri told him. "In Miklagard we had many of them."

"No doubt," Red Beard said and cautioned them to find a place to sleep inside the circle of guards. "They have orders to cut down anything that moves in front of them."

Rafe nodded, and taking Thyri by the hand, he led her away from the fire.

The wine and the nearness of Thyri inflamed Rafe's passion and he drew her to him once they were stretched out under the blankets. He fondled her breasts and put his lips to hers.

And she moved her hand caressingly over the head of his man-thing, while swirling her tongue on the lobe of his ear. "Tell me," she whispered, "has any other woman kissed your man-thing as I have done?"

"No . . . Such pleasure is not a skill among the women of Gumpa's stronghold," he told her.

"There is also a way for a man to do the same thing to a woman," she told him.

"But a woman has only a slit," he replied, using his fingers to spread the lips of her sex.

"A man's tongue, or for that matter a woman's—for it was a woman who first showed me how it could be done—can give much pleasure."

"I want to give you pleasure," he answered.

"Then I will slide over you so that my bottom is close to your mouth. . . . When I begin to suck on your man-thing, you slip your tongue between the lips of my slit."

Rafe was eager for her to begin sucking on him and with ease he lifted her over him, while she pulled up the bottom of her tunic, exposing her naked sex to him.

Immediately, he felt the warm ring of her lips on his man-thing.

She leaned slightly forward and whispered, "Find it, Rafe, oh find it!"

He pressed his mouth against her sex, reveling in the taste of her. Within moments, she was making deep throaty sounds of contentment. Rafe had never before been at a woman that way, and he found himself filled with the urge to devour her. Even the tart-tasting wetness was wholly exciting.

Thyri moved her bottom against his mouth with increasing vigor, while he thrust his man-thing deep into her mouth. Soon each became lost in an ecstasy that dulled the night sounds and brought to their closed eyes a display of color more brilliant than they had ever seen with open eyes.

Rafe could feel Thyri's body tense with passion while in his own the wonderful heat was quickly bringing him to climax. Suddenly Thyri's body trembled and she pushed her sex against his mouth. She shook with passion and taking her mouth away from his man-thing, she uttered a low moan of utter delight. . . .

Rafe reached down and set her again to mouthing his organ. She used her tongue and moving up and down made him groan with delight. . . . His cum rushed from his man-thing into her mouth. He growled with pleasure. Then as he opened his eyes, he watched her slowly lift her head and swallow. Seeing her do that strangely intensified his satisfaction. . . .

XVI

Eventually Red Beard wheeled his column east and after several days of riding, they came to a place where the forest gave way to open plains.

"A man," Red Beard told Rafe, gesturing widely in front of himself, "could ride for days and days before he would come to where the mountains begin."

"Have you been to the mountains?" Rafe asked.

"Once, when I was a boy," Red Beard answered.

They spoke of many things during the time they rode side by side and when they sat across the fire from each other at night. Sometimes they would speak about horses, each giving the other the benefit of his experience with the animal. For, like the Rus, the Khazars were deeply attached to their mounts.

Now and then, Rafe would tell Red Beard about Gumpa. But he would never speak about the stronghold, for fear that Red Beard would suddenly swing his column toward it and attack it. Nor did he speak about Talum, Gumpa's spirit, or Enlil.

Red Beard was not only the leader of his men but also their priest, and in the morning and at twilight he led them in prayers to their god, Jhavh. But he never spoke about Him, though he did tell Rafe that a long, long time ago, his people came from the land of Egypt to where they lived now.

Most of the men in the column knew enough of

Rafe's tongue to be able to speak with him. All of them were friendly, except Garith, who continued to scowl at him, or pretend that he was not there when they rode side by side or sat across from one another at Red Beard's fire.

After two days of going east on the plains, Red Beard again turned north and, that night, he summoned four men to his fire. Each of them brought a pipe and he gave them tobacco. Garith joined them and Red Beard also gave him tobacco for his pipe.

For a while, Red Beard spoke to each one of them, asking about their horses and some of the other men. Then with a characteristic nod, he said, "Tomorrow or within the next few days a caravan will pass this way. It comes every year about this time from the land beyond the mountains."

"And every year," one of the men laughed, "we take a little of what they have."

The others joined in the laughter.

"This year we will take more of what they are carrying," Red Beard said, chuckling with them. And after he explained what he expected each to do with his men, he turned to Rafe. "You will ride with me," he said. "Your woman will remain behind with the men who take care of the asses. She will be safe and should something happen to you, I give you my word she will be taken to her uncle in the north."

Rafe nodded.

Red Beard gave the men wine to drink and said, "I have spent a whole year looking forward to this raid, the last one was so good."

Each of the men boasted he would take more booty this time than the last and when they left Red Beard's fire, Rafe asked, "Where is the caravan going?"

"To the place you Rus call Miklagard," Red Beard answered. "Every year it comes this way."

"I did not know there was anything of value to the

east," Rafe commented. "I always thought it lay to the south, or to the north."

"Not the north," Red Beard said, blowing a huge cloud of smoke in front of him. "The north is a terrible place . . . full of dark forests and cold, even in the summer. But in the south, there is much gold, silver, and other valuables worth having."

"There is gold everywhere in Miklagard," Thyri commented. "I have seen it on the top of their holy buildings and in the houses of the great men. . . . It is said that their god Allah provides them with gold."

Red Beard laughed, "Then perhaps I too should believe in him because he has provided me with gold that should have gone to those who believe in him."

"I do not know," Thyri told him.

"What say you, Rus?" Red Beard asked, looking at Rafe.

"I do not know either," Rafe said.

Red Beard shook his head, the laughter left his lips, and in a quiet voice he said, "Hear O Israel, the Lord is thy God, the Lord is one!" Then closing his eyes, he dismissed them with a flick of his hand.

Later, after Rafe had his fill of Thyri, he lay looking up at the stars. He found the North Star and stared at it for a long time before his eyelids became too heavy to keep open.

Sleep claimed him but not so completely that he could not be visited by dreams. And the one that came to him, or rather the one his spirit found in its night wanderings, was indeed strange. . . .

He was in a place—perhaps a cave—and there were many people gathered there. At one side there was a large table and seated behind it were several men and women.

Rafe sensed something important was about to happen. All of a sudden a man and a woman came forward.

Rafe realized he was at a Thing, a place where some sort of judgment would be given. Gumpa had once told him that all arguments were settled at the Thing.

One of the men at the table said, "Bal asks that the rules be changed. Enlil has no chance of winning Inanna if the game continues as it is now played."

"And what would Bal ask for his son?" questioned the man in the center of the group at the table.

"That he be allowed to kill his opponent and not have to depend on a mortal man to accomplish the task, since all of us know how undependable man is."

"Lord," said the man who came in with the woman, "the game will go on forever. Inanna's power is as strong as mine: What I do, she undoes. . . . The contest is too even to be sport for those of you who watch."

"What Enlil claims is true," another man said.

"And who will speak for Inanna?" asked the man in the center of the table.

"I will," answered a woman from the ranks of those who stood on the sidelines.

"By what right?"

"Enlil's opponent is flesh of my flesh and blood of my blood."

"Then you are his mother?"

"Yes."

"Speak then," the man said.

"I object," Bal shouted.

"She will speak," the man responded in a voice that suddenly became thunder.

"My son is no match for Enlil," she said. "Should you grant Enlil what he wishes he will win, and once again the contest will be no contest."

"And now let Inanna speak," the man said.

"I have helped him only where Enlil has tried to destroy him," Inanna said. "You yourself said I might foil Enlil if I can convince his opponent to follow my word."

"There would be no need for this," Enlil called out, "if she would consent to bed with me."

The man in the center rubbed his bearded chin before he said, "I grant Enlil's request with the stipulation that his opponent now has the power to kill him as well."

"Reject it!" Bal shouted. "You are part god."

"Your death will forever consign you to the underworld," the man said.

"And should I kill him," Enlil asked, "where will he go?"

"If he should fall in battle," the man answered, "then Odin will claim him for Valhalla."

And then one of the other women at the table asked, "How did this start?"

"The way all things start," the man answered, "through the foolishness of a god. . . . But once started it cannot be stopped until one or the other of the contestants is destroyed. That is what the fates have decreed and that is what must be!"

"I will have you, Inanna!" Enlil shouted.

Instantly dark smoke spilled into the place. And it was gone, vanishing with Rafe's sudden wakening. . . . But this time the dream lingered long enough to make him tremble with fear and break into a cold sweat. That he should find himself locked in a life-and-death struggle with a demon was enough to make him quietly moan.

Hearing him, Thyri awakened and asked if he was ill.

"A dream," he said, already forgetting the reason why he had been afraid only a few moments before.

She pressed close to him and said, "Tell me the dream and I will tell you your future."

He laughed softly. "Did you learn that in Miklagard too?" he asked.

She nodded and again asked him to tell her his dream.

"It is gone from me," he said, and put his lips to hers.

Thyri rolled onto her back and opening her thighs, she said, "The camp will soon be stirring. . . . Hurry, mount me . . . Mount me, Rafe!"

Willingly, he did. Soon they became the beast with two backs. And when they finished enjoying each other they fell back breathlessly.

"It is better each time," Thyri giggled.

"Much better," Rafe answered, stroking her naked breasts. . . .

For three days, Red Beard sent riders out from the encampment to scour the country for the caravan. But there were no signs of it. And with each passing day, he became increasingly bad-tempered.

Nothing pleased him, not the food that Thyri prepared for him, or anything his men did, or the presence of Garith. On the afternoon of the third day, when Garith returned from the search, Red Beard railed at him mercilessly, calling him every obscene name that came to his mind.

Then turning to Rafe, he shouted, "Tomorrow, Rus, you ride in search of the caravan and, by the living God, if you find it I will make you my second in command and put Garith at the end of the column to eat dust like the cursed serpent that tempted Eve."

That night there was no laughter in the camp as there had been the previous nights. When Rafe and Thyri finally went to their blankets, Red Beard sat alone staring into the glowing embers of the fire.

"Garith has something new to glower at me for," Rafe commented, as he stretched out on the ground.

"But why should he be angry at you at all?" Thyri questioned.

"I think it is because I was able to break Yggr," he said with a sigh. "Perhaps he tried and failed."

Sleep came to them before passion and by the time they opened their eyes again it was dawn.

After eating some dried fruit and drinking a bowl of goat's milk, Rafe mounted Yggr and was ready to search for the caravan. Three other men were assigned to go with him.

"It must be somewhere out there," Red Beard said, coming up to Rafe. "Find it and I will increase your share of the booty by half again as much as you would have gotten."

"I will take only what is due me," Rafe answered, and turning Yggr's head toward the east, he moved the horse at a walk out of the camp.

The morning passed without any sign of the caravan. By afternoon, the wind swung around from the south to the northwest, bringing with it a cold, misty rain.

Rafe used the camp as the center of an ever-widening circle. They rode all afternoon and toward twilight, when they were well south of the camp, they came to a small river. There they saw the droppings of many horses.

Rafe silently pointed toward the camp. At a gallop they raced back to it. By the time they raced past the guards, shouting as they did, night had already come.

Rafe brought Yggr to a swift halt at Red Beard's fire. The rain was heavier now and it was cold.

"The caravan," Rafe said breathlessly, "is south of here, not north. . . . It is moving west along the course of a small river."

"Did you see them?" Red Beard asked.

"Only the signs of many horses," Rafe told him.

Red Beard glanced at the other men and with a nod

they confirmed what Rafe had said. Then he asked, "How many horses?"

"More than you have here," Rafe told him.

Red Beard roared with laughter and all of the men around him laughed heartily. "Thyri," he shouted, "bring the wineskin for the men. Wine and some food . . . They are hungry and cold."

Rafe and the men who rode with him ate and drank. The wine warmed them and the meat satisfied their hunger.

Red Beard sat and watched them and when they could eat no more, he praised them and said, "Tonight you will lead the rest of us to the river and by dawn tomorrow we will have what we came for." And with that, he shouted orders for the men to assemble. True to his word, he placed Garith at the rear of the column. Rafe rode next to Red Beard.

The wind stiffened and the cold rain stung the men, forcing them to bend low in their saddles. Though the night was as black as Hel, Rafe led the column unerringly to the river.

Red Beard turned west, following the course of the river.

The rain and the wind eased off. As soon as the first gray light of dawn showed in the east, the clouds were pink and yellow.

Rafe pointed to the spoors left by the horses and said, "The rain has washed most of the signs away."

Red Beard nodded and urged the men to keep moving.

When the day finally came, it was gray and the air turned sultry. Soon the men and their horses were weary. But Red Beard gave no indication that he would either slow the pace or halt to rest man or beast.

"They cannot be much farther ahead of us," Red Beard said.

Rafe did not answer. He had heard Red Beard say the same thing many times since they reached the river. He did not know whether Red Beard spoke to encourage the men or himself. But in the past, when he had hunted or raided with Gumpa, he had heard the same or similar words.

The banks on either side of the river narrowed. The water began to flow more swiftly as the horses carefully picked their way along the slender ledge. Several animals shied and almost threw their riders.

They were almost out of the gorge when Rafe looked up to the heights above them and saw Death sitting on an old stump of a tree.

At the same instant a shrill battle cry filled the air. Rocks came hurtling down from the heights above the river.

Within moments riders and horses were screaming in terror.

Missiles thrown from above smashed down on the men and animals. Heads were crushed, backs were broken, and the water near the bank quickly became stained with blood.

Red Beard's column was cut in two.

Before the two halves could join again, the air was filled with the high-pitched whine of arrows.

More men dropped from their mounts into the swift water. Several horses that had been wounded screamed and plunged into the river, hoping to escape the pain that suddenly swept through their bodies.

Red Beard, Rafe, and many others managed to dismount and cautiously worked their way forward along the ledge.

"They will be waiting for us," he said, "once we are in open country again."

"You can be sure of that," Rafe answered.

"We will have to fight our way through them," Red

Beard said. "And then take a wide swing to the east before we return to camp."

Rafe nodded and unsheathed his sword.

Red Beard gathered together the remnants of his force. With the loss of a dozen men and horses, his ranks had been cut in half. The kites and crows were already in the dull gray sky, waiting for the bodies of those who were slain to become theirs.

To the east, twice Red Beard's number were already moving toward him. They rode small, shaggy horses with big heads.

"Tartars," Red Beard said in a low voice.

"They will try to use their arrows," Garith said. "Best to stay low in the saddle."

The Tartars were moving slowly closer.

Red Beard raised his sword. Filling his lungs with air, he shouted, "Hear, O Israel, the Lord is thy God, the Lord is one!" As the words left his lips, the other men picked up the cry and galloped forward.

Rafe was so taken by surprise that he was forced to press after them. He stayed low on the neck of Yggr.

The twang of bowstrings and the eerie song of arrows filled the air. But the arrows missed their mark and one by one they came to earth with a flat thwap.

Soon the thunder of galloping horses rolled over the land. Rising above it were the wild shouts of the men as they rushed toward one another.

"Stay close to me," Red Beard shouted to Rafe. And the next instant, some of his men wheeled off to the right.

The movement took the Tartars by surprise, and expecting the remainder of the men to follow, they swung to head off the few, only to discover the rest of Red Beard's men as they came crashing into their flank.

The first attack brought many Tartars down. But the others turned to fight. Sword crashed against sword. Horses reared and riders slashed wildly to cut each other down.

Rafe fought his way through several Tartars, killing two and wounding the others. His hands were covered with blood and still he slashed at those who were close to him. Suddenly he saw a Tartar bearing down on Garith, as the man was fighting with another one. Rafe rushed toward him and took the Tartar's sword on his own weapon. He fought him until suddenly the Tartar turned and fled.

"Ride," Garith shouted. "Ride!"

The two of them broke free and raced to rejoin their comrades. They were the last to leave the fray. . . .

XVII

Long before Red Beard and his men reached the campsite, they saw the black winged carrion birds wheeling against the gray sky. To be certain they would not be attacked again, Red Beard ordered his men to halt. "We will wait for darkness," he told them, "to continue." And scanning the clouds, he added, "At least there will not be any moonlight."

None of the men answered him. They were numb with weariness. They dismounted and sprawled out on the ground.

Rafe and Garith were nesting side by side. Though they had not spoken a word throughout the long ride, the bond between them had been forged in blood. There was no need for either of them to comment about it.

Red Beard came over to them. He crouched down and, putting a blade of grass between his teeth, he said, "They tricked us into following them."

Garith nodded.

"I do not think we will find much," Red Beard commented, glancing in the direction of the camp.

"The dead," Garith answered solemnly.

"They probably took Thyri with them," Red Beard said, facing Rafe.

"Yes . . . they probably did," Rafe responded sadly. He had enjoyed her immensely. The things she had taught him, he would never forget. . . .

"We will be riding soon," Red Beard told them as he stood erect and walked off.

"He should have known better than to have a woman with us," Garith said in a low, resentful voice. "A woman always brings bad luck . . . I do not know why, but it is so. Women are best off in the stronghold, where they can busy themselves with useful tasks and do no harm."

Rafe nodded. Though he did not agree with Garith, he knew many Rus who held a similar belief.

"Did you know it was a woman, Eve, who brought all our woe into the world and who was responsible for—"

Red Beard suddenly called for the men to mount up.

"Though she was your woman," Garith told him, once they were in the saddle, "Red Beard should not have brought her with us. He should have sent her back to the stronghold."

"If you had said something—"

"Red Beard should have known," Garith answered with a flick of his hand. "He should have known."

There was nothing Rafe could say that would change what had happened, and for fear that he might endanger his hard-won friendship with the man, he chose to remain silent. Like the Rus, the Khazars had their own ways, and if Red Beard went against the ways of his people he would have to answer for it.

The men approached the campsite on foot, holding the reins of their mounts short, in case the animals, smelling death, would suddenly try to bolt. They moved quietly, whispering to their horses to steady them. Now and then an animal snorted.

"Nothing is stirring," Red Beard said.

The asses had been killed; the horses were gone. Those who had been left to guard the site had been killed. All of the supplies had been taken. And there was absolutely no sign of Thyri.

Some of the dead had their bloody man-things stuffed in their mouths. Others had been used as men would use women. All of them had been killed.

Red Beard beat his chest and wailed. He called to his God for help. All of his men did the same. Then they dug holes in the earth, lowered the bodies into the holes, and covered them with the soil until each grave was marked by a mound of earth.

Red Beard prayed over the graves in the tongue of the Khazars. When he was finished with the funeral rites, he ordered his men back into their saddles. And long before the night had passed, they were galloping north again.

"Where are we going?" Rafe shouted to Garith.

"Back to the stronghold . . . If I know Red Beard, he needs some time to lick his wounds and find some other way to give the king his tribute."

"How far is the stronghold?"

"Ten days' ride . . . Soon we will swing east again."

When morning came, they stopped to rest the horses and themselves. The day was bright and the blue sky was dotted with puffs of white clouds.

Rafe lay back in his saddle and, closing his eyes, found himself thinking of Thyri and the enormous pleasure she had given him. . . . He hoped she had been delivered to a master who would treat her well. . . . Then he slept. . . .

Red Beard's stronghold was very different from Gumpa's, where the people lived in solid houses built of wood and stone and were safe from attack behind a stout palisade on three sides and the river on the fourth.

Here the people lived in large shelters made of

skins and wool stretched tight over the trunks of bent saplings. Red Beard's tent was the largest.

From what Garith told him, Rafe learned that Joseph was the king to whom Red Beard paid tribute, and that he lived in a large stronghold made of stone far to the south.

"Only by paying tribute," Garith told him as they sat outside of his tent, "does Red Beard have the right to raid along the river. . . . He and all of the men in this stronghold give the king a tenth of what we gain. It is the law and we obey it. Much of what we would have taken from the caravan would have gone to the king. . . . Now we will have to find some other way of paying our tribute, or he will send his soldiers after us."

Most of the time Rafe took his dinner with Garith and his mother, though now and then he was invited to join Red Beard and his family, which consisted of two wives and two concubines, what Rafe's people would call thralls. He had several children: two who were men and one daughter, who had recently become a woman, and would soon marry.

Red Beard was a generous host and, from what Rafe could see, an even-tempered man to everyone who lived in his tent. He reminded him of Gumpa, though Red Beard spoke more openly about his God than Gumpa ever did about Odin.

Then one night after they had drunk a great quantity of wine, Red Beard said to him, "The king will soon expect his tribute and there is little to send him."

"I have seen herds of sheep and cows," Rafe said, and suggested the very best of them be sent to the king.

"That will only cause him to be very angry," Red Beard answered, shaking his head.

"Perhaps not."

Red Beard nodded. "I know," he said. "The king is

my brother. All of the members of my family put more value on gold and silver than on anything else. I must give him something of great value, or he will send his soldiers to put me and everyone else here in chains."

"I will try to think of something," Rafe responded, staggering to his feet.

"It must be soon," Red Beard cautioned, "or it will be too late."

"Soon," Rafe told him, and on wobbly legs he made his way to the tent that had been given to him. Sleep came quickly to him and though he experienced many dreams, he remembered only the one that came just before he awoke, when he again felt the warm circle of Thyri's lips around the shaft of his man-thing. The pleasure was real and very intense. As he moved to leave his sleeping place, he realized he had spent himself.

With each passing day, Rafe saw the change in Red Beard. He became gaunt and his gray eyes became more veiled. He seldom spoke and when he did, it was to some unseen being. Often he rode out of the stronghold and did not return until twilight had come. It was soon whispered about that Red Beard was possessed by an evil spirit, what the Khazars called a dybbuk.

Then one afternoon, when the summer was almost at an end, Red Beard called Rafe to his tent. He bid him sit and had his oldest wife make the syrupy black coffee that came from Miklagard and also had her serve balls of well-baked dough dipped in honey.

Rafe saw his host was clear-eyed and more like the man he had met on the day Baugi had brought them together.

Red Beard sniffed at the coffee and nodded his head. "It is one of the finer smells in life," he said with a laugh. "Coffee, good wine, the coming of rain after a long drought, and the perfume of a beautiful woman."

"The smell of battle is good also," Rafe added.

"But not of the dead."

Rafe agreed with that.

"Out there," Red Beard said, waving his hand toward the north, "is a herd of wild horses and with the herd is a pure white stallion."

Rafe cocked his head to one side. "I did not know," he responded.

"No one does," Red Beard said with a smile. "But the herd is there."

"How do you know?"

"Because I saw it in a dream," Red Beard answered. "I saw myself astride that white stallion. . . . But I am wise in the ways of dreams and know that it was my brother, the king, who was really astride the white stallion, and by knowing this I also know that if I were to send the horse to him, he would gladly accept it for tribute."

"But you yourself told me that gold and silver—"

"He will accept the stallion!" Red Beard said fiercely. "The worth of such an animal far surpasses the value of the gold and silver I could have given him."

Realizing it was wiser not to take issue with him, Rafe silently sipped his coffee, though it no longer tasted as good.

"Have you ever dreamed that you were riding a white stallion?" Red Beard asked.

"Yes," Rafe admitted with a nod.

Red Beard smiled evilly. "It is clear," he said, "that you were destined to capture the white stallion in my dream."

Rafe shook his head.

"Capture the white stallion," Red Beard told him in a low urgent voice, "and you can continue north. . . .

You will have fulfilled your special purpose. When we were brought together, I told you that you would have a special purpose—I felt it then but now I know what it is."

"And suppose I fail?"

'You will not . . . But if you do, I will send your head to my brother."

"Again you give me no choice."

"Again I give you the only choice that matters," Red Beard said.

"But to find a herd that not even you have seen—"

"I have seen it . . . I have seen it!"

Rafe finished his coffee and was about to take his leave, when Red Beard said to him, "I know where the herd is . . . I know. . . ." Then closing his eyes to slits he warned Rafe against trying to escape. "I do not want to kill you but I will if you drive me to it."

Rafe acknowledged Red Beard's words with a nod and he left his tent. The warmth of the sun felt good and he wandered down to a small river that was not too far from the stronghold. He did not remember much about his dream, other than his riding of the white stallion.

Desolated by what lay ahead of him, he sat on the bank of the river, chewing on a blade of grass. He had heard of many men who, having followed their own dreams, soon found themselves hopelessly lost. The danger of following another man's dream was even greater. . . .

A green frog suddenly hopped into view, stopped, and looked up at Rafe.

He expected it to leave just as quickly as it had come. But it did not and, opening its mouth, it croaked loudly. To Rafe, it sounded as if the frog were scolding him. That idea was so foolish he began to laugh.

Surprised that the sudden sound did not frighten

the frog away, he stopped laughing and hesitatingly called out, "Talum . . . Talum, is that you?"

The frog continued to croak, but the more intently Rafe listened the more certain he was that he heard something like the sound of laughter.

"Talum," he said, sure that if she could have turned into a crow, she might also have the power to become a frog. "I must capture a white horse if I am to be allowed to continue north."

The frog began to hop around and, still croaking, it suddenly vanished into the reeds that grew profusely on the bank of the river.

Rafe shook his head and, getting to his feet, he walked slowly back to the stronghold. He was beginning to think that Red Beard was indeed afflicted with a dybbuk. . . .

XVIII

"When I was younger," Red Beard said to Rafe, who rode silently at his side, "I could have been king of the Khazars, since I was the eldest son. But my father, may he rest in peace, saw fit to pass over me and give the throne to my younger brother. . . . What do you think of that?"

With a shrug, Rafe answered, "If I were you, I would have fought him for the throne."

Red Beard laughed and slapped his thigh. "I thought you would say something like that. . . . But then it would have been brother against brother and such a situation would spread out over all of the kingdom so that many brothers would be at war with each other. Whoever would have gained the throne would have had great difficulty washing off the bloodstains."

Again Rafe shrugged.

"It does not bother me to send tribute to my brother," Red Beard said.

"But you are afraid of his anger."

"He is the king and his law must be followed. . . . Tribute must be given and no exceptions made. . . . If our places were reversed, I would expect tribute from him and if he did not send it, I would have him put in chains."

"I would rather settle the matter once and for all,"

Rafe told him, setting his hand on the hilt of his sword.

"Our way is to use the law," Red Beard said.

Rafe did not reply either by gesture or by word. From Garith he had learned that the law was very important to the Khazars. They had many, many laws; even laws that told them what they were permitted to eat and how they were to treat a woman when her monthy blood flows.

"These laws," Garith had once told him, "have come to us from Moses and to him from Jhavh. They are sacred. . . ."

To speak with any man about those things in which he believed and you doubted, was, Rafe had come to learn, utter foolishness. Therefore, as he had not pursued the matter with Garith, he did not pursue it with Red Beard.

For three days they rode north. On the fourth day, they swung east and rode another two full days in that direction. When they made camp for the night, Red Beard said, "We do not have far to go before we find the herd."

"I hope we find them soon." Rafe's tone was surly. "I want to be on my way north again as soon as possible."

"In good time," Red Beard said, adding a few more sticks to the fire.

Rafe looked up at the night sky. A silver crescent moon hung low in the east and here and there streaks of light suddenly blazed among the stars. Rafe found himself wondering how Thyri had fared at the hands of the Tartars. He sorely missed the pleasure she had given him, and he sighed disconsolately.

"Why so sad?" Red Beard questioned.

"I was thinking of Thyri," he answered, "and all the things she had taught me."

"You will find another woman," Red Beard told

him. "You are young and should not have any difficulty."

Rafe nodded and said, "I also find myself thinking about all the things that have happened to me."

"With regret or with pleasure?"

"I do not know . . . But I am anxious for the future."

"Most men are, but when it comes they are not content with it."

Rafe sat up and locked his hands in front of his legs. "I always seem to be on the verge of remembering something that is very important," he explained.

"Impatience!" Red Beard responded, dismissing the young man's words with a wave of his hand. "I remember feeling that way too when I was your age. But as I grew older, the feeling lessened. . . . Perhaps as a man grows older he learns that he cannot waste time thinking about what could happen and is only interested in what has happened or what is happening."

Rafe stared into the fire, hoping he might see Gumpa again. But he saw nothing.

"Here," Red Beard said, "smoke on this for a while." And he handed a small pipe to Rafe.

"What is it?"

"The juice from a flower that grows in the place you Rus call Miklagard," Red Beard answered. He picked a burning ember out of the fire and lit his own pipe. "You will feel much better and, for a while at least, know all the answers to your questions."

Rafe sniffed at the small bowl. He drew back quickly from the sharp scent.

"It is meant to smoke," Red Beard chuckled, "not to smell."

Rafe picked up a piece of burning wood and set it to the top of the pipe. The smoke went up in a white, sweet-smelling cloud.

"Take several deep puffs," Red Beard counseled.

Rafe did so.

"You will soon feel much better about everything," Red Beard assured him. "Lean back on your saddle, smoke, and look up at the sky."

Rafe stretched out and with the back of his head resting on the saddle, he continued to smoke. The stars suddenly began to move, very slowly at first and then faster and faster until they were no more than whirling fragments of light.

"Tell me," Red Beard asked, "what do you see?"

Rafe smiled. He knew that Red Beard was speaking to him but the words were indistinct, as if they were coming from where the stars whirled around.

"Think of the white stallion," Red Beard said. "Think of the white stallion."

Rafe blinked and moved his eyes down from the sky to the wavering flames of the fire. On the other side of the flames was—

"The white stallion is master of the herd," Red Beard said. "I have seen him in a dream just as you will soon see him. . . . Come let us go together and look at him."

"How will we go?" Rafe questioned.

"We will ride . . . We will ride until we find him."

Rafe mounted Yggr and, with Red Beard at his side, he went in search of the white stallion.

"We will find him," Red Beard began to sing, "where the tops of the mountains brush against the sky, where the chasms are deep; we will find him where the forest leaves fly, where the pathways are steep."

Rafe sang Red Beard's words and their voices vaulted to the sky and then swiftly plummeted to earth, splashing multitudinous colors through the night into the morning sky, before the first flash of the yellow sun appeared above the seam of earth and sky.

They rode swiftly, but not swifter than the sun rolled from east to west and daylight gave way to night and night to daylight.

"There, there," Red Beard shouted, pointing to the river in front of them. "The mountains lay beyond. . . . See—just gray shadows in the distance."

Blowing smoke across the wild water, they galloped to the opposite bank. Then they raced toward the misty mountains.

Sometimes they slept, but never for long. They ate and drank little and stopped only to rest their horses. They themselves could have continued to ride without interruption.

The mountains drew closer; the land under them was hard with rocks and scarcely anything grew on it. The sun burned them; the rain drenched them. Summer became autumn. The nights were cold and the days turned gray with the promise of snow.

Sometimes they galloped past someone and Red Beard would shout a hallo but never wait for a response.

Rafe saw no one he knew.

The snow came and with it the wolflike bite of the wind. The snow was deep and the cold burned their fingers and faces.

They reached the mountains and led their horses through the narrow chasms until they rode once more into spring.

"The forest," Red Beard shouted. "The forest, there in the distance, where the trees are tall and straight."

Rafe puffed hard on his pipe and took the lead in the race to find the white stallion. The forest was dark but full of bits of sunlight. Some were huge shafts that pinned the earth and sky together, while others were flat, like strips of beaten gold that reached from branch to branch and tree to tree.

Three whole days they rode through the forest before they came to its end and the beginning of a plain that stretched to where the blue sky touched the green earth and as they marveled at the vast distance in front of them, Rafe could hear the thunderous beat of many hoofs.

"The herd," he whispered. "I can hear it."

"I hear nothing," Red Beard said, shaking his head, "other than the wind in the grass."

"Listen!"

"Only the wind in the grass," Red Beard repeated. "Where are we?"

"At the end of the forest."

"Where the white stallion lives."

"Where our dreams are met; where we are!"

"There . . . There . . . The herd comes—the herd comes . . . See where the green dust rises . . . See!"

"My dream . . . My dream . . . My dream."

Rafe spurred Yggr and galloped to where the green dust floated between the blue sky and the surge of the herd.

The white stallion led the herd. He was larger then any horse Rafe had ever seen; perhaps even as large as Odin's eight-legged Sleipnir. He stopped when he saw Rafe, and pawing the ground with his huge front hoofs, he made the earth fly out from under him. He was as white as snow, as white as milk, as white as the puffs of clouds that gathered above the earth.

Rafe patted Yggr's neck and he whispered softly to him, lest he take fright and suddenly bolt. "I will capture and break him," he said, "just as I captured and broke you."

Yggr whinnied.

"Yes," Rafe said, "I will be careful." Looking up at

the sun, he saw much of the day was still left. "If I capture him this afternoon, then by evening I will be able to ride him."

Again Yggr whinnied.

Rafe moved closer to the white stallion. Its eyes glowed with a dark carbuncular light and it violently shook its head.

Yggr halted and trembled.

Suddenly the white stallion reared up and, wildly flailing the air in front of it, the beast snorted fire.

Yggr reared and shied away.

But Rafe brought him around again to face the white stallion.

"Beware, beware," Yggr's whinny told him, "he will singe your hair and burn your flesh."

"And I will master him," Rafe answered. "I will have him on the end of a tether and lead him where I will."

The stallion reared again and blew long tongues of flame from its quivering nostrils. Then it turned and galloped off.

"Now," Rafe shouted, spurring Yggr. "After him!"

The huge white animal raced across the open land and after it thundered the herd. Wherever the stallion's hoofs struck stones, showers of sparks burst in the air. He ran and ran, moving now to the east, suddenly veering to the west, to the north, and then shifting to the south.

No matter which way he turned, Rafe followed.

The sun moved low in the west. Fierce red and orange came into the sky and lingered until purple trailed in from the east, bringing night.

In the darkness that came, there was no crescent moon or stars. The only light came from the white stallion and the flames he breathed.

As the night became deeper, the darkness thickened. Rafe could feel its strange, terrifying weight. It pressed upon his chest and filled his mouth and nose. But he would not slow his pace, though the distance between him and his quarry never lessened.

More than once the white stallion swung its head around to look at Rafe and then with a snort of flames turned away and continued to run.

Many of the horses in the herd could not continue to run and slowed to a walk, or burst their hearts in a vain effort to keep up with the white stallion.

Rafe looked for the coming of dawn in the eastern sky but no light showed through the thick blackness.

Yggr began to tire. The animal was lathered and foaming at the mouth. His flanks heaved.

"Run," Rafe urged. "Run, we must not let him get away."

Yggr leaped forward. The distance between the hunter and the hunted diminished, slowly at first and then with ever-increasing rapidity.

The white stallion suddenly turned. Rearing up, with its great hoofs ready to strike and flames coming from its trembling nostrils, it was ready to fight.

Rafe rode Yggr around and around the white stallion in an ever-contracting circle.

The beast snorted fire and charged.

At the last instant Rafe swung Yggr away but the next moment he raced back and with a rope in his hand, he managed to put the loop over the head of the white stallion. He pulled the rope tight. The loop grabbed the beast's neck.

The animal screamed in rage but with the voice of a man. Within an instant, the white stallion changed its form and Enlil was fighting to free himself.

Rafe lost no time. Quickly he snared the demon's feet. Leaping from Yggr's back, he circled Enlil several times with the rope, drawing it tighter and tighter with each turn. Then he knotted it so that it would take several strong men many hours to untie it.

Enlil shouted at him and though he used all his strength to burst the bonds, the rope held him fast. "I will kill you," he shrieked. "I will place your head on the tip of my sword and throw it at Inanna's feet." As he screamed, his body became covered with scales and blood dripped from his mouth.

Rafe remounted Yggr and without looking back at Enlil's writhing body, he galloped away, not knowing in which direction he was going. But soon a small line of light appeared in the darkness. A great wind blew up. Huge chunks of blackness were blown away, leaving patches of blue sky.

From the distance, Rafe heard Red Beard calling to him. He brought Yggr to a halt, and looking toward the Khazar, he shook his head.

Red Beard was still caught in the smoke of his own dream. He had not moved from where Rafe had left him when he had started to chase the white stallion.

Rafe turned toward the north; he was free of Red Beard's dream, free of his own dream too. . . .

Rafe found the river again and took time to water and feed Yggr. The animal had served him well and he was grateful. "In time," he said, "I will find you a mare and you will sire many colts."

Yggr whinnied.

"I will not go back on my word," Rafe assured the animal.

When they started north again, Rafe thought about his adventures with Red Beard. Part of it seemed to have been the work of the fates but much of it could be laid to Enlil, who sought his blood for reasons he did not understand.

Then looking back from where he had come, Rafe shouted, "Hear me, Enlil . . . Hear me . . . I will not let you take my blood without trying to take yours. . . . I will be your enemy, since you declared yourself to be mine."

Enlil spewed up darkness in the eastern sky and made the earth tremble until cracks opened in the stone cliffs and giant trees came crashing down.

Rafe shook his fist and laughed defiantly. He moved Yggr into a trot. By nightfall, he came to a place along the bank of the river where several huge stones were placed upright. Seated with her back against one of them was the crone, Talum.

"You took a long time to get here," she said.

He was too happy to see her again to notice her pouting. He leaped from his horse and ran to her. A moment later he lifted her high above his head.

"Put me down!" Talum yelled. "Put me down."

He set her on the ground.

"I thought you would never come," she told him. And before he could answer, she told him she was hungry.

Rafe went off to hunt and quickly returned with a small boar.

Talum ate greedily, sucking her fingers when she had finished with the meat. Then she asked him for water.

He brought her some from the river. And when he sat down again, he said, "I looked for you . . . but you had already left."

"I could not wait for you," she told him.

"Then why were you waiting for me here?" he questioned.

"Because," she said, "another three days' ride from here and we will have reached the end of the river."

Rafe could not believe he was so close to it.

"And where will we go from here?" she questioned.

"To the island of Zurd, where the jarl Vikar lives."

"But why there?"

"It is a long story," Rafe answered. "But I will tell it

to you in good time." Then, looking straight at her, he asked, "Did you change yourself into a frog?"

"A what?"

"A frog . . . I saw one that stopped and scolded me."

Talum cackled.

"Was that you?"

"A crow, yes . . . Sometimes a dog, other times a wolf . . . But never a frog . . . I hate frogs, toads, snakes, and lizards."

Rafe nodded. Knowing a witch woman was surely a strange experience.

"I will sleep now," Talum said, moving away from the fire to the base of one of the stones.

Rafe sat by the fire. All that had befallen him gave him much to think about. Though he was not quite sure why or how, he knew he had changed; he hoped he had become somewhat wiser. . . .

XIX

Rafe and Talum traveled north for three days along the bank of the river. Sometimes she rode with him on Yggr; other times they walked with one of them on each side of the horse.

Rafe told her what had happened to him when he had reached the bottom of the chasm: his fight with Lars, how he was captured by Baugi and brought to Red Beard, the chief of the Khazars.

Talum never made a comment, or nodded that she heard him. At first Rafe was annoyed with her lack of interest and said as much, adding, "I do not know why I am telling you anything, since you would not even wait for me to come up out of the chasm."

"I have already waited for you too long," she answered in a strange, faraway voice.

"When I returned to where I had left you," Rafe insisted, "you were not there."

Talum shrugged but did not answer.

The leaves were turning from their summer green to yellows, oranges, reds, and many shades of russet. The sun was quick in its flight across the sky but not so quick as it soon would be. There was a chill in the air even during the day and the wind began to show its fangs.

The closer they drew to the mouth of the river, the more people they passed. Some, like themselves, were travelers and others lived in well-made houses along the way. Often they saw Viking ships returning from Miklagard.

The morning of the second day dawned with a gray sky. A filigree of hoarfrost lay on the ground and on the splendiferously colored leaves.

Talum complained about the cold and said, "I am not used to it . . . I do not like it one bit."

Rafe reminded her that he had found her in the midst of a terrible blizzard.

But she ignored what he said and continued to grumble about the cold.

The third night, when they sat in front of the fire, Rafe asked Talum if she could tell him why Enlil was his enemy. "I do not understand why he should want to kill me," he said in a sad voice.

"Enlil wishes to people the world with demons," she answered. "He would bring them forth from the body of Inanna and the race of man would perish at their hands. All would be chaos again."

"But what have I to do with that?" Rafe questioned, extending his hands toward the flames to warm them.

"You must answer for your father's actions."

"But what did my father do? . . . Who was my father? . . . What did he do?"

Talum shook her head.

"Please tell me, if you know," Rafe implored.

"It is not for me to tell," she responded. "In your doing of what must be done, you will discover how it all started." Without saying anything else, she left the fire and went some distance away to sleep.

For a while, Rafe puzzled over Talum's words. Having bested Enlil once, he was no longer as fearful of him as he had been. But he was not so foolish as to think that he was as powerful as Enlil. He took a deep breath. Looking at Talum, he wondered how much of her magic had been involved in his success over Enlil.

With that question in his head, Rafe stretched out and fell into a deep sleep. Sometime during the night, he suddenly awoke—or he dreamt that he was awake and standing over Talum. . . . To his astonishment, she was no longer a crone, but had transformed herself into a lovely olive-skinned woman with long raven hair. She was asleep. He stood there looking down at her for a long time. She was strange, yet familiar. He had seen her several times before. But he could not remember where. Perhaps in another dream . . .

To Rafe it seemed that he had just begun to look at her when the first light of the new day began to show in the east. He returned to where he had been sleeping and lay there with his hands behind his head, looking at the stars as they faded, first one by one, then in whole groups, until finally all of night vanished.

Suddenly the clamor of wild ducks flying south roused him from a sleep that left him as soon as it had begun, or so it seemed. He sat up, rubbed his eyes, and looked toward Talum. The hag was not in her place. Scrambling to his feet, he called to her.

She answered from the edge of the bank. "Since you were asleep," she said, "I decided to catch a fish or two for breakfast." And she waved two good-sized trout, one in each of her bony hands, in front of her.

Where the river poured into the sea, there were many houses, many more than Rafe had ever seen. All of the ships that traveled between the sea and Miklagard passed there.

The banks of the river were crowded with Vikings, Rus, dark men from Miklagard, and Tartars from the east. There was much bartering going on and gold and silver passed through many different hands.

A great many scents were carried by the wind. Some were of food but others were sharper and cleaner; these came from the open sea, where the white-crested water rushed toward the land with a thunderous roar.

Rafe found the places between the houses crowded with people. A large, pock-faced man shoved Talum aside with such force that she landed hard against the side of a wagon.

Rafe shouted after the man as he helped Talum to her feet, "It is easy to do that to an old woman but would you do it to me?"

The man whirled around. There was murder in his green eyes. With a growl, he answered, "To you, or anyone else who gets in my way."

A crowd of men, women, and children quickly gathered to watch.

"Who are you?" the pock-faced man demanded.

"Rafe . . . And the old woman is Talum."

"And do you know who I am?" the man bellowed, his face turning red with anger.

"I know you push old women aside," Rafe responded sharply.

The man nodded and, drawing his sword, he said, "When I am done with you, I will have your tongue on the point of my sword for your insolence."

Rafe drew his sword.

The circle of spectators drew back.

The combatants rushed toward each other. Their swords came together with a fearful crash that made both blades shiver. They separated.

The pockmarked man wearily circled Rafe, feinting to one side and then the other.

But Rafe guarded himself and with quick slashing strokes forced the man to dance away, lest he feel the bite of Rafe's sword.

Though the day was gray and cold, with a brisk wind coming off the sea beyond the headland, Rafe and his adversary were covered with sweat.

Some of the men in the crowd shouted, "Get him, Gylif; show the Rus how to fight."

Others championed Rafe and yelled at him, "Teach Gylif a lesson . . . Teach the bully a lesson."

Back and forth Rafe and Gylif went; each one of them growing more and more determined to best the other.

Gylif thrust and scored Rafe's arm with the point of his blade. A stream of blood marked the wound.

Despite the cut, Rafe's pace never slackened. He was ferocious in his attacks, strong in his defense.

For an instant, Gylif was off his guard.

Rafe bored in and drove his weapon hard into the man's belly and a moment later pulled it free.

A look of astonishment appeared on Gylif's face. He dropped to his knees. Blood drenched his hands. When he opened his mouth to cry out to Odin, the god's name was drowned in a fountain of blood. He toppled forward. For a few moments his body trembled; then it was still.

Off to one side, in the shelter of a house, Rafe saw Death. When Gylif fell, Death moved slowly past the ring of spectators. He stood close to the stricken man, waiting for his spirit to join him. But Gylif's spirit was reluctant to follow Death and he was forced to place a rope around his neck and drag him along.

As Rafe watched Death and Gylif's spirit march slowly toward the sea, several men were already shouting, "A Rus has just killed Gylif."

A number of Vikings came running and within a short time, Rafe and Talum were completely surrounded and ropes were set upon them. They were roughly pulled to a large ship and dumped into it.

"Where are we being taken?" Rafe shouted to the steersman.

"To Vikar, the jarl of this land . . . Gylif was kinsman to him on his mother's side."

161

Rafe looked disconsolately at Talum. "I had hoped to come to Vikar in better circumstances than these," he said.

Talum nodded and closed her eyes.

XX

The ship carrying Rafe and Talum reached the island of Zurd at night. They were taken from the vessel and by torchlight swiftly conveyed to a dungeon in a stone building, where they were unbound only to be chained to the wall by their legs.

As soon as they were alone, Rafe suggested to Talum that she leave. "You can change yourself into a bird," he said, "or perhaps a mouse, and be gone before I am brought to Vikar."

"I will stay," she said, "and give testimony on your behalf."

"The Vikings are swift and savage in their justice," he responded.

"I am tired and need to sleep," Talum told him, stretching out on a pile of straw.

Rafe leaned back against the cold stones of the dungeon wall. He was hungry and missed the presence of Yggr, for whom he had developed much fondness and respect, especially after the stamina the animal had shown in the fight against Enlil, when he was the white stallion.

"Yggr will be fine," Talum assured him from her pallet of straw.

Rafe uttered a wordless grunt. Then drawing up his knees, he placed his arms over them and lowered his head. Within a very short time he was asleep, dreaming of Thyri's warm embrace. But just as he was about to experience the ultimate delight, the stout door that sealed them in the dungeon banged open.

Four men stood in the doorway; two held torches and two entered the cell. One went to Talum and the other to Rafe. With a key they opened the locks that held the chains on the prisoners.

"Where are we going?" Talum asked.

"To stand before Vikar, the jarl of this land," one of the men answered.

Rafe and Talum followed the two men with torches and behind them came the other two, with their swords drawn.

The light from the torches cast long shadows on the stone walls. Now and then they passed a place in the wall where a door of wood marked another cell. Behind some doors there were mournful sounds; behind others there was only silence.

They were taken through a narrow underground passageway, where the stones were wet with water and their footfalls echoed dully. Here and there a rat scurried out of their path only to stop a short distance away and look at them with gleaming yellow eyes.

They climbed a steep flight of narrow steps. The flames of the torches were bent backward by the strong breeze. The air was suddenly filled with the sharp, clean scent of the sea. They were led along a parapet and though the night was too black for them to see the sea, they could hear its terrible roar on the rocks below. Finally, they entered Vikar's great hall, which was noisy and ablaze with torchlight. Instantly, the hubbub ceased and all eyes went to them.

Vikar's table was at the other end, where a huge hearth was tended by several thralls. The scent of food and drink was so heavy on the air it made Rafe's mouth water.

From every side there were murmurings of disapproval. Neither Rafe nor Talum gave any indication they heard them. But Rafe whispered, "We have been judged without having been heard."

"Vikar will do the judging," she told him.

When they reached the table, one of the guards ordered, "Kneel before Vikar, the jarl of Zurd."

Rafe remained upright, his eyes fastened on an old man with a hoary beard, a nose like an eagle's beak, and eyes as blue and bright as a summer's sky.

The guard put his hand on Rafe's shoulder, but he shook it off.

The men at the tables raised their fists toward Rafe and shouted, "Force him down; make the Rus kneel before Vikar!"

Again the guard tried to push Rafe down, but this time Vikar waved him aside and in a strong voice that belied his age he said, "Gylif was my kinsman."

"That was your misfortune then, Vikar," Rafe responded in a loud voice. "I would not boast of that relationship. . . . But I did know of one about whom you could speak with pride and his name was Garth, your brother."

"Half-brother," Vikar corrected, now more suspicious of the prisoner than before. "But how do you know him?"

Rafe shook his head. "We must settle the business of Gylif first," he answered.

"Perhaps my knowing more about my brother might have saved your life?" Vikar suggested peevishly.

Lately Vikar had been plagued by nightmares, a sudden quickening of the heart by day and, worst of all, the growing premonition that disaster, like a wolf, was waiting to spring at him with the dawn of each new day. Now standing before him were strangers who could be the harbingers of all that he had come to fear.

"If I live it will be because Gylif deserved to die!"

A roar of disapproval rose from the people at the other tables.

"Let him speak," Vikar shouted.

Instantly there was silence in the great hall.

Rafe nodded and quickly explained what had caused him and Gylif to fight.

"And the crone with you was the cause of what happened?" Vikar questioned.

That Vikar referred to Talum in such a derogatory manner bothered him, and Rafe said, "She is my grandmother and skilled in ways unknown to most who claim to be masters of magic." He spoke in such a tone that all who listened would know his anger.

Vikar pursed his lips. "Perhaps," he suggested, "your quick tongue gave offense to Gylif?"

"I said no more than I told you I did," Rafe said, suddenly fearful of his own boldness. He was gambling with his life as well as Talum's, though Vikar would have a difficult time killing a witch woman.

As if he knew what Rafe was thinking, Vikar moved his eyes to Talum and asked, "What have you to say to all of this?"

"No more than has already been said," she answered.

"And what of your magical powers?" the jarl asked, his brow wrinkled with intense concentration.

"It should not have been mentioned," Talum answered, looking askance at Rafe. "But it is more than some possess and less than others."

"I have soothsayers, Granny, who read the stars and others that read the future in the blood liver of a cow. . . . And I have priests who can call upon the gods for many things and spaewomen who can summon the spirits of those who have gone to Valhalla or to Hel. . . . Can you do as much?"

Talum's wizened face splintered into a toothless smile. Pointing the bony forefinger of her left hand at the man sitting to the right of the jarl, she exclaimed, "A rabbit or a stag!"

Instantly, the man became one and then the other.

The great hall was suddenly filled with shouts of dismay.

"Or here snow," she said, pointing her finger down to the floor, "and there rain." Snow came to where she and Rafe were standing and on the far side of the hall it was raining.

Vikar rose to his feet and shouted, "Enough . . . enough . . . You have proved your power."

With a wave of her hand, Talum took away the snow and the rain. The stag became a man again.

The jarl sat down again and said to Rafe, "Tell me your name."

"Rafe . . . And my grandmother is Talum."

"From what you have told me," Vikar said, "Gylif was killed in a fair fight and I will not take your life for his."

Rafe looked at Talum and then smiling up at the jarl, he warmly thanked him.

"But since you took the life of one of my men," Vikar told him, "I demand that you render me some sort of payment."

"We have nothing. . . . All that we had was taken by your men when they took us captive and then the only things of value were my horse, Yggr, and my weapons."

"Some restitution must be made," Vikar insisted.

"I have nothing."

"There is yourself," Vikar said. "Agree to serve me and—"

"For how long?" Rafe questioned.

"A year."

Rafe was about to agree but Talum spoke first. "A year is too long," she said. "But for the length of time it takes to make one voyage to Miklagard."

"Done!" Vikar exclaimed. "And half of all Rafe gains will go to Gylif's woman."

Rafe agreed to the terms and the jarl offered him a flagon of mead to seal the agreement. When each of them drank from it, Vikar asked if they were hungry.

"Famished would be more truthful," Rafe answered.

Vikar and his vassals laughed and chairs were put at the table for Rafe and Talum. Each was given a generous portion of freshly roasted venison, good bread, and boiled cabbage.

"Now tell me how you happened on my half-brother?" the jarl asked. "Tell me all."

Rafe told him everything, commented on Garth's bravery and how Ragnar was lost, and on Lars's treachery.

"And what of Thyri, my niece?"

"Taken by Tartars," Rafe told the jarl. He went on quickly to explain the circumstances of how he had lost Thyri. "It was she who told me about you," he said. "We were going to come here together."

Vikar nodded and from every corner of the hall there were murmurs of wonderment about the things they had just heard.

"I have nothing more to tell," Rafe said.

"There is one thing more," Vikar responded. "You did not say what caused you to leave your stronghold and come north."

"My destiny," Rafe answered.

"Did you show him his destiny?" the jarl asked, fixing his attention on Talum.

She was so busy eating that she neither heard the question nor was she aware that he was looking at her.

Vikar repeated what he had said, only this time he used her name.

"I have come north to find out about my mother," Rafe said.

168

"Do you think she is here, in the north?" Vikar asked.

Rafe shook his head. "She was killed before she ever arrived here," he responded sadly. "I passed the place where it happened on the river, far to the south."

Vikar pulled on his hoary beard. For a few moments, he said nothing.

The great hall was very quiet now. The older men looked questioningly at each other.

Then Vikar asked, "When was your mother killed?"

"A long time ago," Rafe responded. "I was but a child."

Suddenly Vikar slammed his fist down on the table with such force that everything on it jumped up and fell back with a clatter. "Must I pull the words from you?" he shouted. "Tell me all in one fell swoop."

"I was no more than a babe in her arms when it happened," Rafe said, thinking to himself that Vikar's humor changed as frequently as the wind shifted.

"And yet you know what happened?"

Rafe shook his head. "When I reached the place on the river I knew it had happened there," he told him quietly.

"What else do you know?"

"Only that my mother was from Miklagard and she was on her way north to marry—" Rafe could not get the other words out of his mouth; they would not go beyond his lips.

"She had already borne a child and yet she was going to marry?" Vikar questioned in a low, raspy voice that would have become a thunderous shout had he lost control of it.

Rafe nodded.

"To whom was she going?"

"I do not know."

"And who was the father of the child?"

"A god," Rafe whispered, suddenly remembering the conversation between his mother and the Viking.

"Louder . . . I cannot hear you."

"I seem to remember that a Viking said a god had lain with her."

Vikar began to tremble and foam came from his mouth. His face turned purple but when several of his men offered him help, he waved them away. "Your mother," he said, having difficulty speaking, "was coming here to my stronghold . . . to me, to be my wife. The ships I sent to bring her here from Miklagard never arrived. . . . After a time I went to look for them and found them on the bank of the river far to the south of here. I found the charred remains of the ships and close by were bones of my men and Nikona, the woman who was to be my wife."

"I do not know what to say," Rafe told him, repeating his mother's name to himself.

"You have said too much," Vikar said. "You have told me things I did not want to know." He looked at the men who were seated on either side. "Even my vassals cannot look at me; they sit with downcast eyes and think me a fool. . . ." Suddenly he was pounding on the table. "But I would not have had her to wive . . . I would have sold her to someone who—" He finished with a violent wave of his hand.

Vikar called for his attendants and left the table, saying, "I will have to think about this . . . I will have to think about all of this. . . ." Then turning to Rafe, he asked, "Tell me why you were not killed with the others."

Rafe glanced at Talum.

"Tell him," she said.

"When I was put in the fire," Rafe explained, "the flames drew away from me. Gumpa, seeing this happen, rushed into the midst of the flames and pulled me out."

The hall was suddenly filled with angry shouts. "He is lying," many of the men yelled.

"And then what happened?"

"Gumpa took me and raised me as one of his sons."

"Where is Gumpa now?"

"Dead."

"How did he die?" Vikar asked. "I hope in a way that prevented him from entering Valhalla."

"I killed him," Rafe said.

The hall suddenly erupted in a frenzy of angry shouts. Many men called for the opportunity to fight Rafe. Nothing, in their eyes, was more heinous than for a son to kill his father and in their eyes Gumpa was Rafe's father.

"I will decide what is to be done," Vikar roared, his voice louder than all of the others. "I will decide." Then looking at Talum, he said, "What have you to say, Granny, about all that you have heard?"

"Only that it is true," Talum answered.

Vikar nodded; then he ordered the night at end. Quickly the torches were put out. The men either went to their own houses to sleep or found a place in the great hall to spend the remainder of the night.

Rafe and Talum stretched out near the hearth. Bathed by its warmth, they quickly fell into a deep sleep.

For several days Rafe and Talum enjoyed the hospitality of Vikar and though he never once made mention of anything that had been told to him on the night of their first meeting, he was almost always surly, especially if Rafe asked questions about his mother. Soon it became apparent to them that Vikar was not pleased with their presence. He could neither disregard nor completely believe all that Rafe had told him. It was also clear that he had little love for his dead half-brother Garth. Some of his men implied that if he were less fearful of Talum's magic, he would have had the two of them killed. Rafe and Talum did not speak about the danger but each of them knew they must do something to remove themselves from it before it completely overwhelmed them.

Rafe soon discovered that Vikar's people lived along the coast. On small farms somewhat inland, another people dwelled. These people were called Fomoiri and the Vikings were sorely afraid of them.

A farmer told him, "They are hairy things, with big chests and stone clubs. . . . They climb down from their lair when the fog comes and stays for a few days, or when the snows come. They carry off our women and children and the weaker men. The women they use; then kill. The children and men are killed and immediately eaten. The women are eaten too but with them they wait a while. . . . I have heard it said that our women are eaten by theirs." He gestured toward the mountains, which were, even on a clear day, shrouded with mist.

When Rafe told Talum about the Fomoiri, she said she had heard the same thing from some of the women to whom she had spoken. Rafe said, "I think I have found a way to gain us our freedom." And the next night he mentioned the Fomoiri to Vikar.

In an instant a silence came to the table and then to the great hall.

"They are our enemies," Vikar said in a low angry voice. "Spawn of Loki and some female demon."

"They guard the boiling entrance to Hel," commented one of the venerable Vikings at the table.

"Are they men?" Rafe asked.

"Not such as you have ever seen," Vikar answered.

"But are they men?" Rafe repeated.

Vikar nodded and said, "They are men."

"Then they can be killed like men," Rafe told him. "A blow from an ax, or a wound from a sword that would kill an ordinary man, only makes them scream with rage. . . . It takes more than one blow and more than one sword thrust to bring a Fomoiri to his knees and even then it is hard to kill him."

"But it can be done?" Rafe pressed.

"Yes . . . But why do you want to know whether the Fomoiri can be killed?"

"What would you give to a man who would end their raids?" Rafe asked.

"A goodly quantity of gold and silver . . . As much as he might fit into a small sack."

"And a promise on your sword that he and whoever he takes with him will not be molested but will be given passage to the mainland?"

Vikar's eyes went to slits. He grasped the direction of Rafe's request and would have denied it if the men in the hall were not looking at him so intently. He nodded and said, "I would agree to that."

"Then I will go against the Fomoiri," Rafe said. "I will take as many of your men as you can see fit to give. But all must be good fighters and not afraid of joining Odin."

"I will not send any with you," Vikar told him. "What you do, you must do on your own without any help from anyone. Even Talum must remain behind until you have completed your task—that is, if you can complete it . . . While you are gone Talum will remain here."

Rafe looked at Talum and he whispered, "I did not think I would be entrapped by a snare of my own making."

"It often happens that way," she replied.

"Will you go alone?" Vikar asked.

"Yes," Rafe answered. "I will leave at first light tomorrow."

"Bring me the head of their leader," Vikar said, drawing his sword, "and I swear that I will honor my word." And he drew the blade over the palm of his left hand, making a thin red line of blood appear. He held the palm of his hand up for all of his men to see.

Everyone in the hall shouted praises to Vikar. He accepted them with a nod and a thin-lipped smile.

"How will I know their leader?" Rafe asked above the noise in the hall.

"No one has ever seen him," Vikar laughed. "No one knows if the Fomoiri have a leader. . . . But that should not stop you from finding him, killing him, and bringing his head to me."

Rafe did not answer; he had truly ensnared himself in an impossible task.

"If after seven days you do not return," Vikar told him, "I will deal with your adopted granny as I see fit. . . . My priests tell me there are ways to deal with a witch woman, ways that would send her to Hel or Utgard, if they would have her there."

At first light the following day, Rafe bid good-bye to Talum. Embracing her, he whispered, "If I am not back in three days, wait no longer. . . . Become a crow and fly away. Do not let them take you."

Talum nodded but did not speak.

Rafe released the crone. Turning from her, he started toward the mountains that in the growing light of day remained towering heights of darkness. He moved quickly inland, setting more than one watchdog to barking as he passed isolated farmsteads.

Light came into the eastern sky, giving the clouds a salmon color that quickly turned yellow and then a solid gray, as the sun rose higher. A cold wind brought a thin rain down.

Rafe quickened his pace. Soon he was looking for a way up. Using his hands, he worked his way from ledge to ledge. Often he would lose his hold on a slippery rock and begin to slide, stopping himself by grabbing hold of another fragment of stone.

His hands were raw and bleeding. Every part of his body ached from the enormous effort of moving from one narrow perch to another. Despite the cold rain, he was covered with sweat.

He paused and looked toward Vikar's stronghold. For all its size, it looked no larger than a child's plaything. Even the great hall was not much bigger than an acorn. Then he moved his eyes upward to where the tops of the mountains were lost in the swirling mist. He shook his head at the dark awesome sight above him and continued to climb.

Through the morning and afternoon the sullen sky never changed, and when Rafe moved into the mist the sky above and the earth below vanished. He was no more than a speck of a man, climbing the black rock face of a mountain. Though in the past he had done many things alone, he had never felt as desolate, as helpless, or as insignificant. It was as if he had spent all of his life on the side of the mountain and the future held no prospect of him ever leaving it. Despite his fears and the melancholy nature of his thoughts, Rafe pulled himself ever upward.

The mist thickened, forcing Rafe to grope for each hold on the rocks above. Then, as he was reaching high above him, there was a sudden beating of wings nearby. He stopped and listened, knowing that he had climbed too close to the nest of an eagle.

The sound was directly above him. He flattened himself against the face of the mountain.

The bird shrieked hideously.

The next instant Rafe was fighting to escape its tearing talons and beak. The air around him thrummed to the beat of the bird's enormous wings. He brought his arms up to shield his face.

The bird screamed.

175

Rafe reached out and blindly tried to grab hold of its neck.

The eagle's talons tore a piece of flesh from his arm.

Rafe lost his footing and almost pitched headlong into the gray murkiness below. But the bird, anxious to tear more of his flesh, pushed him back onto the ledge.

Suddenly the eagle broke off its savage attack, whirred up into the dark mist, and with a terrible shriek plummeted downward at him.

Rafe had managed to loosen his sword. Though the contest was in the bird's favor, he would not suffer defeat without first trying to kill it.

The eagle came screaming down with its horrible talons ready to rip into him.

Blindly he thrust his sword at the oncoming harbinger of death. The blade's point grazed the bird's neck, making it screech with rage and wheel away. Within a moment, the eagle had turned and was coming back for another try. Just as it was again above him, a sudden rumbling filled the air. The huge bird wheeled off to one side.

The next instant a shower of rocks fell from the heights above Rafe. The eagle screamed and disappeared into the black mist. Moments later the mountain began to shake. Huge chunks of earth dropped away in thunderous roars. The top of the mountain glowed red. Streams of fire poured down its side, masking it with red rills of flame.

Once more, the earth trembled and with an explosion louder than summer thunder the entire top of the mountain erupted into huge fiery plumes of yellow-orange.

Rafe pushed back against the rock. Suddenly the ledge under him gave way! He screamed and felt he was falling into the bowels of the earth, into an oblivion of liquid rock, of flames, of earth that heaved and stank of sulfur and death. He tried to stop himself but everything he grabbed to stop his fall went with him. He bounced from ledge to ledge.

He screamed again and again but because of the thundering rumble of earth, he could not hear himself.

And then he stopped falling; he was in total darkness. . . .

The great heaving of the earth ceased and the accompanying thunder became no more than the anger, growl, and tormented screech of rocks grinding against rocks. Rafe could hear these sounds but could see nothing in the tenebrousness that surrounded him.

He tried to move but could not. It was as if the weight of the darkness was beyond his power to overcome. He could not even flex his thumb or forefinger. . . . That he might be dead seemed a very definite possibility, or perhaps he was not yet dead but in the process of dying.

Rafe moved his eyes from side to side to see if Death was standing nearby. But the darkness was too thick even to reveal Death!

He was most certainly not in Valhalla, though he had fought bravely against the eagle before dying; nor was he in Hel, where those who do not fall in battle go. Somehow he had fallen into that place of nothingness between life and death. Terrified he would have to remain there until the end of the world, Rafe struggled against the darkness. But the more ferocious his struggles, the heavier the darkness seemed to become. Exhausted, he stopped. And again he looked for Death, but instead of Death, he saw the faintest bit of white misty light. It was a long way off. But it came quickly toward him.

Even from a distance, Rafe could see the light was either shaped like a man or surrounded the body of a man. The closer it came, the more clearly he saw it.

When it was no more than a few paces from him, he saw that the light and the mist were Gumpa.

"You fought a good fight with the eagle," Gumpa told him with an appreciative nod. "I watched all of it. . . . But you would not have won."

"Enlil?" Rafe asked, suddenly realizing who he really had fought.

"In the form of an eagle," Gumpa said. "He would have torn you to pieces if the gods had not made the earth move."

"Then I am dead?"

"Come," Gumpa said, "come with me." And waving his spectral hand over him, he added, "We must hurry."

The weight of the darkness that pressed down on Rafe lessened and he moved his arms and legs. Within moments he was on his feet.

"We must go farther down," Gumpa told him. "Farther down . . . Follow me . . . Follow me!"

Rafe stayed close behind Gumpa, who said nothing as he led him through the darkness.

They moved along a strange meandering path that Rafe could not see, though he sensed it, as he sensed the multitude of spirits on either side of them who silently watched their progress.

The darkness began to lessen and in the strange, cinerous light, he saw the bodies of men, women, and children writhing under the weight of the demi-darkness. Though they screamed in agony their ululations remained muted.

"Who are they?" Rafe questioned.

But Gumpa would not answer.

They soon left the grayness and came into a place of light, though it was nothing like the sunlight of the world above. The light here was without warmth, without the contrast of a blue sky, or a star-filled night. It was the light that only the dead know.

Gumpa stopped and pointed to a small group of people. "Your mother," he said, "is there."

Rafe looked at him questioningly.

"Here," Gumpa said, "the killer and the killed dwell side by side and though each knows what the other had done, none care. . . . Nikona, your mother, bears me no grudge. Your spear took care of that. Now go to her."

Rafe nodded and hurried to where his mother sat with the others. She was as beautiful as he remembered her to be. Her hair was long and black. Her eyes were sea green.

She smiled at him, and in that smile Rafe recalled the smile of a woman he had once seen in his dreams. He called to her but she did not answer.

She bent to what she was doing.

Rafe moved closer and looked to see what so held his mother's interest that she would not speak with him.

"Watch closely," Gumpa said, coming to Rafe's side.

"She is playing a game," Rafe commented with disbelief.

"Watch . . . She takes the bundle of sticks and throws them . . . Then she picks up as many as she can without disturbing any of the others."

Her opponent was hooded and the spectators who stood around them and watched were specters like Gumpa.

The bundle of sticks passed between Rafe's mother and her opponent many times. The number of sticks held by each increased and decreased as the game continued. Each player became more and more engrossed.

"What are the stakes?" Rafe asked.

Gumpa put his spectral finger over his lips.

From time to time, Rafe saw his mother glance at

him. Though there was a pleasing smile on her lovely face, there was deep concern in her eyes.

"I have played this game too long," the hooded figure said in a sepulchral voice. "I have played too long. One more throw of the sticks for each of us and that will be an end to it."

"One more throw," Rafe's mother agreed, taking up the remaining sticks to cast them down again. She studied the arrangement before making her first move. Then swiftly and carefully she picked up one after another, until there were nine left. She paused and looked at the way the sticks lay. To move one would disturb the others and thus she would give her opponent the opportunity to win. She reached for a stick and nimbly plucked it away from the rest of the sticks without moving them. Again and again, she performed the same remarkable feat.

The specters gathered closer.

Rafe was sure that if they had the gift of breath, they would have been taking deep breaths, as he himself was doing.

Then suddenly his mother's hand faltered, trembled, as she went to lift a stick from the remaining three. The other two moved.

"Mine!" the hooded figure shouted gleefully. "Mine!" He took the bundle of sticks from her and tossed them to the ground. Quickly he gathered them one at a time. When there were only three left, he taunted, "I must win . . . You know that . . . I must always win." He snatched up each of the remaining sticks with startling swiftness. "I have won," he shouted. "I have won." Then pulling back the hood, Death revealed himself.

"Run!" Rafe's mother shouted. "Oh, my beloved son . . . Run . . . Run to the opening in the rocks . . . Run . . . Run . . ."

"He is mine!" Death shouted.

"Run my son . . . Run . . . Run . . . Run!"

Rafe whirled around. He was already running back toward the heavy blackness, when he heard his mother cry out. Looking back over his shoulder, he saw Death cast her among those tormented spirits who were doomed to writhe in agony until the end of the world, when the monsters would devour the gods. . . .

Rafe ran into the darkness, stepping on the twisting, tormented bodies of those who were imprisoned there.

Death came behind him, shouting that he had won him.

The darkness was heavy and liquid. Rafe brushed against slimy serpentine creatures. Many tried to coil themselves around his legs but he managed somehow to pull himself free.

Huge batlike creatures with red glowing eyes and teeth of fire came whirling out of the darkness. But he beat them off.

He ran, hoping to outrun Death, knowing that if he escaped this time, he would fall to him the next.

The darkness seemed to go on for ever and ever. Rafe's strength was ebbing; he could feel it flow out of his body the way sand once ran through his child-like fingers. Here and there flames suddenly leaped out at him. But he continued to run.

And then a hot wind came that scorched his lungs.

"You will not escape me," Death shouted.

Rafe forced his legs to pump harder. Then suddenly in the distance he saw the opening in the rocks. Sunlight washed across the top of it. He flung himself forward.

A catlike claw tried to stop him. He grabbed at it and flung it back into the blackness.

Breathless and exhausted, he was within striking

distance of the opening, when Death hurled himself at him. Rafe stumbled and fell.

"I have you!" Death cried exultantly. "I have you!"

Rafe gathered all his remaining strength and with one gigantic effort hurled Death away from him. Scrambling to his feet, he clambered up the rocks to the opening above. Death was at his heels.

Within moments Rafe pulled himself into the sunlight, leaving Death below. The sunlight blinded him. He closed his eyes, and when he opened them he found himself looking into the dark-bearded face of a Viking. Behind him was the sun and the blue sky.

"I thought you were dead," the Viking said.

Rafe nodded and whispered, "I thought I was too."

"My name is Thorolf," the Viking said.

"I am called Rafe," he told him and, closing his eyes, he slept. . . .

XXI

The night was bitter cold and the northern sky was filled with turquoise and white light.

Rafe sat across from Thorolf at a cooking fire. Two other men were there: Svein, a young man with brown eyes and brown hair, and Egils, a priest of Odin, whose eyes were blind. All of them were wrapped in thick skin cloaks that protected them from the fierce cold. All around them were the cooking fires of other men.

Rafe was ravenously hungry. He had slept through what had been left of one day, all of the night and the following full day and night. He tore off great mouthfuls of venison but drank sparingly of the proffered mead, so that he might keep a clear head when he spoke to those who were giving him shelter and food.

When all had their fill of meat and allowed much time to pass between sips of mead, Thorolf asked Rafe how he happened to be where he had been found.

"I had climbed up out of the opening," Rafe answered.

"An opening to where?" Egils, the priest, questioned.

Rafe explained how he had fallen from the mountain when the earth moved.

"Are you a young man?" the priest asked.

Thorolf laughed and said, "An old face, Egils, with graying hair but a young body."

Rafe touched his face and ran his fingers through his hair. He looked at Thorolf and said, "I am twenty, or perhaps no more than twenty-two years old."

"Fifty would be my guess," the Viking responded.

"Tell me more about what happened to you," the priest asked, having difficulty keeping the sound of his voice even.

Rafe told him everything and then he asked where Vikar and his people were.

"Vikar and his stronghold were taken by the earth," Thorolf said. "Where the stronghold stood now stands a newly made hill. . . . And as for what you have told us, I only know that I myself pulled you up from a huge hole and though I could not be sure now, then I was certain that I heard shouting from below. . . . You were more dead than alive and your left arm was badly wounded."

"The eagle tore a strip of flesh from it," Rafe explained.

"Then you were with Death?" the priest asked.

"He and my mother played sticks for my life. He won and would have taken me, but my mother shouted a warning and I was able to escape."

The priest made a whistling sound while Thorolf and Svein shook their heads with disbelief. Then Thorolf said, speaking in a low voice, "I would have had you tell us something else."

"But what I told you," Rafe replied, "is true."

"I believe him," Svein said, speaking for the first time. "I do not think a man could make up such a story."

"What do you say, Egils?" Thorolf asked, looking at the blind priest.

"I have never known a man to look at Death and

not die, yet he claims not only to have looked at him but also to have escaped him."

Rafe shrugged but did not speak.

"No one is here to gainsay him," Svein said. "If he is lying it will be sure to come out in everything else he does."

Rafe liked the young man and appreciated the effort he was making on his behalf.

"Then you would have him sail with us?" Thorolf asked.

"Yes," Svein replied. "I am sure he will prove his worth."

"And you, Egils, would you have him too?"

The priest nodded and said, "If the gods are against him, we will soon know. . . . Let him sail with us."

"Sail where?" Rafe asked.

"Out to the open sea, to Miklagard . . . We were on our way there when we saw the earth heave under this island and came ashore to see if there was anything worth having. We found you and nothing else."

For a few moments, Rafe thought about Talum. He hoped she had managed to escape before the earth began to move.

"What have you to say?" Thorolf asked.

"I will sail with you."

"And will you fight, when it comes to fighting?" the Viking asked.

"Yes, I will fight."

Thorolf slapped his thigh and, laughing loudly, shouted the news to the men at the other cooking fires. Quickly they gathered around him. They toasted good fortune to Rafe and drank much mead. . . .

Rafe sailed in Thorolf's ship, the *Gull*. His place at the oars was just forward of the helmsman, who was Svein. There were two other ships: the *Serpent* and the *Hawk*. Each vessel was dragon-prowed and a huge image of that fire-breathing beast decorated the sail. The ships were well provisioned and each man was armed with a good bronze sword, a spear, a bronze battle-ax, a knife, and a shield of hard leather.

Rafe learned that Thorolf was a jarl in his country and that most of the men had sailed with him before. He was told Svein was related on his father's side to Thorolf's father.

When night came, Rafe ate dried fish and drank mead to wash away the salty taste. When he lay back against the side of the ship to sleep, he thought about his adventures. His descent into the realm of the dead and subsequent escape was much to consider. . . .

That he had been outwardly changed by it, he no longer had any doubt. Once, he had chanced to look at his reflection on the polished blade of his sword. All that Thorolf had described he had seen. He appeared much older and besides the wound on his arm, his face bore the scars of the eagle's beak. The experience had marked Rafe in a way that set him off from other men. The men on the ship spoke to him with a peculiar kind of deference. Though he was sure they knew none of the particulars of his experience, they sensed that he was different from them.

Rafe hoped the outward changes he had undergone were reflections of inner changes that would give him the wisdom to know his destiny when he saw it, since he knew many men did not have that capacity.

These burdensome thoughts made Rafe sleepy. Closing his eyes, he listened to the hiss of the sea as the hull of the ship sliced the waters. Soon he slept and spent the remainder of the night in a deep, untroubled slumber.

Within a few days, Svein told Rafe they had turned south and soon would be running along the Frankish coast.

Since the ships they were sailing were not raiding vessels, Rafe asked why they were going to Miklagard.

"For gold, for booty," Svein answered. "The Moors in Iberia and on the coast of Africa have much gold and silver. We will take it from them and then go to Miklagard to buy some of the things we need. . . . By spring we will start back along the rivers until we reach the northern sea. By then we will be well loaded with treasure.

Rafe was contented with the answer and did not ask any more questions.

Two days along the Frankish coast, the gray sky suddenly turned black and a cold wind that blew froth off the tops of the waves came howling down from the north. Within moments the sea became a surging mass of giant black waves with white crests.

Thorolf and Svein were at the helm, fighting the sea to keep steerageway. The sail boomed and the mast went down with a sharp snapping noise. Thorolf ordered it cut away and it was heaved into the surging sea.

The ship struggled to the crest of a wave and then it slid with sickening speed into the trough. A huge wall of water loomed up in front of them. The men pulled at the oars with all their might.

Ever so slowly the ship began to climb the gray wall in front of it but when it almost reached the top, it dropped back. The wall of water broke over them.

Men screamed. Oars snapped. The ship was tossed in one direction and then another.

Rafe managed to hold onto his oar. A man came swirling toward him. It was Svein. Just as the sea was about to carry the helmsman away, Rafe let go of his oar, grabbed hold of the man, and pulled him back onto the ship.

"Thorolf is gone," Svein shouted, breathing hard. "We must get to the helm or the ship will go down."

Without a word, Rafe started to claw his way toward the helm. Svein was with him.

The sea washed over them but they fought their way to the helm. Each took hold of it and, using all their strength, they pushed against it to free the ship from the terrible grip of the sea. Pitting their strength against the sea, they managed to steer the ship into the wind. Svein shouted to those who could to use their oars. The ship held its way. It crested wave after wave. The storm blew itself out the following morning and when the sea moderated, Svein looked toward the other ships. They had suffered less than the *Gull* but each of them had lost several men overboard.

The ships turned into a small cove and worked their way some distance up a small river. There they were beached. Lines were made fast between them and some nearby stout trees.

Then the men made camp, built fires to warm themselves, ate, and slept.

Rafe wrapped himself in his bearskin cloak, stretched out close to the fire, and found himself thinking about Talum. . . . Then he slept and dreamt once again about a beautiful olive-skinned woman. . . .

Snow fell during the night and in the morning there was ice on the river. The Vikings were forced to chop their way through it and put to sea again, since they feared their ships might be trapped by the ice. If that happened, they would be forced to haul them overland to the ocean or to spend the winter in the land of the Franks, who were their enemies. By acclamation of the *Gull*'s crew, Svein was appointed its captain and he in turn chose Rafe to be his helmsman.

The sea and sky were gray. The land in the distance

was almost black. They sailed day after day without a pause.

They sailed south into milder weather, blue water, and clear skies. At night the ships found refuge in a cove or a short distance up the mouth of a river. Food was abundant, from all kinds of meat and fish to fruits and fresh vegetables. Time was taken to repair the ships and let the men rest. Most of their faces were quickly turning to the color of well-used leather.

Svein taught Rafe how to navigate by the stars, the loadstone, and the bearing plate, which when used properly would reveal how far south they had gone. Rafe learned quickly and his skill soon exceeded Svein's.

Rafe and Svein became good friends and now and then they would talk about their lives: their pasts and sometimes the future.

Svein had been to Miklagard twice before and he assured Rafe that nowhere else were the women as beautiful, or as willing to bed with a man. He told him about the food, the magnificent buildings, and wealth that was everywhere. "And nowhere else," he said, "are the men so wise; they have runes that every man can read."

Rafe told his friend about Red Beard and the Khazars, but made no mention of his experience with the white stallion, or what he had learned about his mother from Vikar, or anything about Talum.

Svein hoped he would gain enough gold and silver on this voyage to buy his own ship when he returned home. "I want to lead my own men on raids," he said. "And when I have enough gold and silver, I will marry, buy land, and only go raiding in the summer, the way men of means do."

Rafe said he was searching for something, but he never revealed what it was.

As they went south, they saw more and more ships.

But they were always too far away from them to attack. Still, the men spent much of their idle time preparing their weapons for such an eventuality. Swords and knives were finely honed; spear- and arrowheads were made secure to their shafts; and battle-axes were ground down to a good cutting edge.

The men peered anxiously at each new sail they sighted, knowing that one day in the near future they would be close enough to strike. They had the same wide-eyed look of anxiousness Rafe had seen on the faces of Gumpa's men whenever they had gone on a raid. He himself must have looked that way once. He had always been eager to go on a raid with Gumpa but now he was not at all pleased with the prospect of having to fight.

Often he would look at the sail in the distance, where the sea and sky come together, and find himself hoping the ship would disappear over the rim of the earth before Svein and the other captains took up the chase. That he had lost his taste for fighting, or worse, his courage, was a source of deep concern to him. He had never really known anything else but fighting. As for his valor, he nor anyone else had ever questioned it. But now he could sense the difference and wondered if in some way it had something to do with the change he had undergone in the place that lies between Hel and Valhalla.

For the next three days, the *Gull* and the other two ships crisscrossed the sea near the narrow strait they had come to, hoping to find a richly laden trading ship. On the evening of the third day, two sails appeared in the west.

Svein ran forward. With one arm wrapped securely around the dragonlike bow, he peered intently at the sails. By the time he shouted they were coming toward them, the men on the *Gull* were eagerly straining at the oars to reach the quarry before night came.

None of the three ships raised sail, though they had a good wind at their stern. A sail would have betrayed their presence and they wanted to be in for the kill, before the men on the other two vessels realized their position.

The men rowed with unbelievable speed. The long ships skimmed the darkening water, while in the distance the two vessels grew larger and larger.

Rafe held a straight course.

Svein stood close to him, his sword already drawn.

Suddenly from across the water they heard the frantic shouts of the Moors. Within moments, the two ships began to turn.

"The chase has begun!" Svein shouted, leaping from the stern deck. "Raise sail! Raise sail!"

Four men shipped their oars and immediately began to hoist the mast into place and pull up the sail; it caught the wind with a thunderlike boom. The men went back to their oars.

Rafe glanced at the other two ships; each had its sail set. The three of them were racing toward their prey.

The merchantmen were also running before the wind. The overseers shouted at their galley slaves to row faster.

The Vikings' ships bore down on the Moorish vessels. Soon they were only a few lengths of cable behind them.

Night came. The sky was resplendent with stars. A yellow crescent moon rose in the east.

"The *Gull* will go between the two ships," Svein shouted to the other captains. "Put us between them," he said to Rafe. "See, they are already trying to prevent it from happening."

The two Moorish vessels drew closer to one another.

"Row," Svein shouted, "row!"

The men pressed themselves. Even though they increased the *Gull's* speed, it was not enough to place her where Svein hoped to have her positioned.

The enemy ships had put lines between them. Before Svein could order his men to backwater, the prow of the *Gull* became snared on the first line. Still moving forward, she carried the second and third one. Within moments, she was wedged firmly between the two enemy ships.

Instantly the Moors swarmed aboard the *Gull*, while her crewmen rose up to meet the challenge.

Rafe released the helm. Unsheathing his sword, he leaped into the fray. The air was filled with shouting, and then the screaming of the wounded and the dying.

The men from the other two Viking ships joined the fight. Blade clashed against blade.

The decks of all the ships were wet with blood. A blade flashed and a man lost an arm, or found himself stumbling over his own guts.

Rafe fought hard. He warded off many killing strokes. Wet with sweat and breathing hard, he followed the surge of the Vikings onto the deck of one of the Moorish ships. He saw Svein and the next instant the sudden slash of a scimitar took the man's head from his shoulders and carried it until it fell beneath the feet of the men.

More and more of the *Gull's* crew were killed or wounded.

The men from the two other Viking ships fought to break the wall of Moorish seamen. But each time they rushed them, they were driven back with heavy losses.

The Vikings shouted to Odin, while the Moors yelled, "Allah Akbah!"

Once Rafe chanced to look at the black waters of the sea and he saw they were roiled white by the swift movements of sharks.

The combat moved back to the *Gull*. The Moors were pressing their remaining men very hard. More and more of the crew passed through the doors of Valhalla.

Rafe slashed out at all of those who came against him. He was splattered with blood and blinded by his own sweat. His right arm was weary and his hand ached from holding the hilt of a sword for so long.

Suddenly a sheet of flames broke from one of the enemy ships. The screaming became louder. The Moors on the other ship cut the lines, freeing the *Gull*. She drifted away from the other vessels.

The men aboard her fought from side to side, from stem to stern until the last of the Moors were killed. When that was done and the deck was littered with bodies and severed limbs, Rafe was the only survivor. Exhausted, he dropped to the deck. He saw neither a sail nor a smudge of smoke in the early-morning sky.

Wearily Rafe got to his feet. One by one, he put the dead men over the side, until the sea around the ship was alive with sharks. Then he drank some mead, stumbled to the stern sheets, sat down, and wondered how long he would be able to survive before the sea claimed him for its own.

"Not long," he said aloud. "Not long!" Then climbing up to the deck, he took hold of the helm. With the aid of a slight wind, he pointed the *Gull*'s bow to the east, to where Miklagard lay. . . .

XXII

At the mercy of the wind and the currents, Rafe spent days wallowing on a flat, mirrorlike sea. At other times, he was fearfully tossed about by demented waves and currents.

The mead soon gave out and the water quickly followed. He chewed leather to bring moisture to his mouth. Then chewed it because he had nothing else to eat.

The sun burned him almost as black as the Moors. The lack of water swelled his tongue, blurred his eyes, and dulled his wits. He saw Death standing in the bow of the ship and would have crawled to him, but lacked the strength.

Day after day the *Gull* drifted one way and then another. She was a derelict ship with no place to go. Other ships came close but none close enough for a member of their crews to see that there was still a man aboard her.

Sometimes Rafe saw the ship and tried to call out, but his swollen tongue would not form the words and he lacked the strength to lift his arm and show that he was still alive. The night came and gave him some respite from the hot glare of the sun. But as the darkness deepened, he would be reduced to a shivering, teeth-chattering child, who wept until the first rays of the sun once again warmed his trembling body.

More than once he looked over the side of the vessel. In the depths of the clear water he saw the silver-gray forms of the sharks who were following him, knowing that if they waited long enough he would be theirs.

To end his agony, Rafe thought about letting himself drop over the side. . . . In a trice the sharks would dismember him. The pain would be sharp but it would soon be over. He would not have to suffer as he was suffering in order to live. . . . But each time he thought of ending his ordeal, he would also see the darker form beyond the sharks. Though his brain was sun-scorched, he knew that Enlil was there in the depths of the sea waiting to watch the sharks tear him apart. Perhaps he even waited to join them in their frenzied attack upon him.

One evening the blue sky grayed over and before night came torrents of rain fell.

Rafe lay back, opened his mouth, and let the rain pour into him. Every part of his body drank. As soon as his immediate thirst was satisfied, he forced himself to collect some of the fresh water in the hollow of what had once been the sail and transfer the precious liquid to a water skin for future use.

The rain continued all through the night and into the next morning, when the clouds began to dissolve and a huge rainbow arced across the sky.

Revivified by the water, Rafe made a simple fishing line. Using bits of leather for bait, he caught several fish and ate them raw. With his hunger somewhat assuaged, he took the helm again and brought the ship back to its former course.

From time to time, he caught a glimpse of land in the distance. But he lacked the means to bring the *Gull* closer. The land always remained a gray smudge on the distant horizon. . . .

A few days after the life-restoring rain had fallen,

Rafe was again without water. But this time he drew the moisture from the raw fish he ate.

With nothing else to do but stay at the helm, he found himself going over the events of his life. His destiny seemed to be as remote as it ever was and seeking it had made him look old long before his time.

Rafe began to wonder if all men who sought their destiny were, as he was, caught in a conflict between two gods. . . . If that were so then neither a man nor a woman had anything to say about what the gods did to them in pursuit of their own ends. . . . Whenever his thoughts tended to move in the direction of the gods, he looked over the side of the ship.

The sharks were always there and so was the dark, amorphous shape of Enlil.

More than once Rafe became so angry, he shouted down at the demon, "Come here on the deck of the ship and fight . . . Come here and fight!"

The dark shadow always grew darker and once the sea rose up with stormlike fury, even though the sun was bright yellow in a cloudless sky. But the sea subsided just as quickly as it had risen up.

And once a flight of gulls passed noisily over the ship. Looking up at their wheeling forms, he shouted to them, "Would that one of you were Talum!"

But none of them was she and, screeching they flew on their way.

Talum was never long out of Rafe's thoughts. Though she was no more than a crone, he held her in high regard. She was far wiser than the men he had known. Albeit she was terribly ugly, she had always been kind to him and on several occasions she had saved his life. That she was a witch woman no longer bothered him and aloud he said, "I could make good use of her conjurations now. . . . I could indeed."

Day after day, the *Gull* continued to drift eastward. Storms came and battered the already wounded ship.

But she weathered them, and when the sun returned to the sky or stars Rafe worked the vessel to sail east again, to sail toward Miklagard.

Rafe lost track of time. The progression of the days and nights became meaningless. Sometimes he slept during the day, lashing down the helm to hold the *Gull* on course. Then at the first chill of evening, he would awake to remain so throughout the night.

Day and night, he thought of Gumpa and the stronghold, his adventures and, very often, about the black-haired, olive-skinned beauty who with each successive dream was becoming more and more real.

He saw fewer sails and much less of the gray smudge on the horizon that marked the place where the land lay. It became difficult for him to distinguish between his dreams and reality.

There were even times when he grabbed hold of his sword and rushed wildly from bow to stern, thrusting and slashing at imaginary enemies, fighting the Moors once again.

But Rafe also experienced quiet times, especially when the sea was calm and rocked the *Gull* gently in her soft embrace. Lucid during these intervals, he knew that he could not continue to drift much longer. The *Gull* had sprung several leaks and the bow was already lower in the water than it previously had been.

Rafe realized that a good part of the time he was possessed by spirits who robbed him of his wits. He knew there was a possibility that during one of those sieges, he would inadvertently go over the side. Should that happen, the sharks and Enlil would make quick work of him. To prevent this, he lashed himself to the helm and hobbled his feet.

He seldom looked toward the bow without seeing Death waiting for him. Once, Rafe shouted to him, "I will not go with you easily, as I have seen so many others go."

With a laugh, Death answered, "Whether you come with me easily or hard makes no difference. You will come; everyone comes. . . . It is the same for everyone; there are no exceptions."

But Death did not venture to extend his bony hand. He remained seated in the bow with his black-hooded cloak draped around him, regardless of whether the sun was bright and hot or the night was cool.

"Tell me," Rafe questioned, speaking to Death as he would have to an old friend, "since in the end all mankind wind up in your place where none is more kingly than you, what is the reason for us to come unwilling and screaming into this world and leave it the same way to enter your domain?"

"I do not know," Death admitted. "What happens, happens; I am only doing what I must do. . . ." Then with a shrug, he said, "I have often pondered the same question, only to arrive at the conclusion that there is no answer. . . . In the beginning, it started that way and no one has found the way to stop it. I see nothing wrong with it other than that I am sorely maligned for doing what the gods decree."

Rafe smiled and with a nod said that he sympathized with him. Then he added, "I think your bad reputation comes from the violent way you approach those you take."

"But that is just it," Death demurred. "I come only after the violence has been done. Disease precedes me, surely war does, and so does anger. Someone must be there to make things right. I think of myself as a cleanser; I take those who no longer are capable of maintaining life's struggle."

Rafe slapped his thigh. He admitted that he had not thought about him in quite that light. "But if what you say is true," he responded, "why then are you waiting for me?"

"Your life should have been mine when your mother lost the game of sticks," Death said. "I am only waiting to claim what is mine, nothing more."

"What about the sharks and Enlil?"

"How you come to me is entirely up to you. Most men, if they would come of their own accord, would immeasurably lessen their suffering. But they are afraid. . . ."

"With good reason," Rafe countered. "Once they follow you, they cannot change their mind and return to the world of the living."

Death shrugged but did not disagree.

Whether his conversation with Death took place at one particular time, or whether it continued over many days and many nights, Rafe did not know or care. His association with Death was one of long standing. Unlike most men, he had frequently seen him and now that Death had become his companion, he was grateful, if for no other reason than that he had someone other than himself to talk to. And perhaps, even more important than the diversion Death provided, was the strange transformation he underwent in Rafe's eyes. No longer was he the hooded skeletal figure that Rafe had previously seen in their various encounters. Now he was a handsome young man, with a bland, almost innocent face and depthless blue eyes.

"You have become younger during our talk," Rafe chided, "and I have become older."

"Not older," Death told him, "but very much wiser . . ."

Suddenly Death vanished and the sky turned gray. The air was filled with loud voices, speaking a language Rafe did not understand. Hands were placed upon him and he was taken from his place near the helm to a rower's bench, where his hands and legs were shackled.

Though his vision was blurred, Rafe could see some of the other rowers. A few were black but most were white. The stink was enough to make him gag.

An order was shouted. A drummer started to beat time. The air was rent by the crack of a whip and then its snakelike hiss.

An instant later Rafe's back felt the stinging bite of the leather strip. His body jerked upward but was held down by the shackles.

Another searing stroke cut across Rafe's back. He cried out and, grabbing hold of the oar, he bent his body to it.

The whip came down on the backs of other rowers. They groaned in agony.

The beat was maintained until darkness came. Then it was slowed and food and water were passed to the galley slaves. For the first time since he had been taken aboard, Rafe had the opportunity to raise his head and look around. There were oil lamps on the upper deck and on the mast. The catwalk where the overseer maintained a vigil on the crew was not illuminated.

The man next to Rafe was black but the one in front of him was white. He spoke in his native tongue, giving him his name. The man answered, telling him, "I am called Olaf. . . . Several of my shipmates are on the other benches."

"Whose ship is this?"

"I do not know. . . . There is a captain, whose name is Al-Tartushi, from Cordova. He stays on the stern behind us. I know no more."

After a few days at the oar, Rafe discovered that there were several other Rus aboard, that they had been taken captive by Vikings traveling on the river and sold several times before they became the property of Al-Tartushi.

There were many Moorish seamen and soldiers aboard the ship but the most hated by the galley slaves was Ibn Fadlan, the overseer, who it was rumored had once been a Viking himself and chose to follow the ways of Allah. Fadlan was a huge, muscular man with a drooping mustache, a bald head, and small, ratlike eyes.

Because it was necessary, if Rafe wanted to avoid Fadlan's wrath, he quickly learned the language of the Moors. Soon he was able to speak to the black man next to him, whose name was Dubi and who had been a galley slave for as long as he could remember.

Rafe asked, "Has anyone ever escaped from the galley?"

Dubi shook his head and, gesturing with it to Fadlan, he answered, "None from this ship, not with him on the catwalk."

Many times the ship went into battle against other vessels. The Moorish soldiers fought well and died hard. Often during a fight with another ship, several of the oars would splinter and the men at them would be chained to a huge piece of wood.

Rafe's arms grew very strong from pulling at the oar. He was quickly recognized by Fadlan as one of the strongest rowers aboard the ship. He was also one of the very few Rus or Vikings who could speak the language of the Moors.

The galley sailed into a harbor, where the slaves were quickly transferred from the ship to a large prison made of stone with stout wooden bars across the windows, which were too high for the men to reach, even if one stood on another's shoulders.

The prison stank as badly as the galley and, like the ship, there was no hope of escape from it.

None of the men knew where they were, though

some guessed from the look of the guards they might be on the island of Sicily. But others maintained they were farther east.

Within a few days of their arrival, several of the men sickened and quickly died. Rafe, Dubi, and two Vikings were chosen to carry the bodies to the wall and throw them into the sea.

The light outside the prison was blinding. But from the parapet, Rafe could see the harbor was not very big. Several ships were at quayside. A few of the buildings were made of stone but most were wood. The place was more like a stronghold than a city, which had been described to him by a few of the galley slaves.

The sea beneath the wall was filled with huge boulders on which great waves broke with a thunderous roar.

When Rafe and the other men were finished with their grisly work, they were herded back to the prison. But he had seen enough to speak to all of the slaves about the possibility of escape.

"We need only to force our way out of here and seize two ships: one to escape in and one to block the entrance to the harbor."

"We would be cut down before we ever reached the ships," one of the oldest of the slaves said.

Many agreed with him.

"At least," Rafe countered, "we would be dying like men."

A great number of heated disputes broke out and when night came, nothing was settled.

Two days later, three more men died.

Rafe, Dubi, and the two Vikings were called upon to remove the bodies. Knowing that he would never unite all of the galley slaves to make an attempt to escape, he told the men with him that he was going to hurl himself into the sea and attempt to swim clear of the wild water directly beneath the parapet.

"You will die," Dubi told him.

"Then that is my fate," Rafe answered.

The guards prodded the four slaves with their spears, shouting for them to hurry.

Outside, the sky was a sullen gray. The air was heavy with the promise of rain.

The two Vikings pitched the first body over the wall and were immediately hustled back to the prison for the third dead man.

"I will go with you," Dubi said in a low voice as they lifted their burden over the wall.

"Now!" Rafe shouted. Letting go of the dead man, he leaped up on the wall and dove into the water below. The wind whistled in his ears. From above him, he heard the startled shouts of the guards.

Within moments, Rafe crashed into the surging sea. The water closed over him. It was warm, almost comforting. He let himself go deep, very deep, and when he touched bottom, he righted himself. Looking up, he saw Dubi arrowing down toward him. At the same time, he saw the gray bodies of sharks dart and twist as they tore huge mouthfuls of flesh from the bodies of the men who had been cast into the sea.

With lungs aching for air, Rafe swam to the surface. The waves pounded against the rocks. Breathing hard, he fought to keep himself from being dashed against the huge boulders. Swimming hard, he pressed against the fury of the sea and swam free of the incoming waves. He paused to fill his lungs with air. Looking behind him for Dubi, he did not see him until a wave lifted his black body and dashed it against a white rock.

Rafe began to swim again. He was some distance from the shore when he sensed another presence. The possibility that sharks might be close by made him redouble his effort. But still the presence persisted. Finally he glanced over his shoulder.

The triangular fin was there, following him! He started to swim, but this time with less speed. Now and then he paused long enough to look over his shoulder.

The fin seemed closer.

He faced the shore. It was too far from him to offer a place of safety. Besides, if he did reach it, he might be captured the moment he reached the beach. A runaway galley slave was punished by flogging or castration. To be whipped by another man would make him less of a man and castration would leave him no longer a man at all.

Above him the sky darkened. Lightning flashed, cutting jagged rents in the black clouds. Then Thor's hammer crashed against the earth.

The sea god, Njord, brought a fierce wind from the south that whipped the water into unimaginable wildness.

Rafe was tumbled by the waves as if he were no more than a leaf being blown about by an autumn wind.

He fought the sea but he could not hold his own against its mighty power. The waves were too much for him to fight. His strength waned. His arms and legs ached. He tried to float but the heave of the sea was too much for him.

Then suddenly he again saw the triangular fin. It came at him. He lacked the strength to take one more stroke. He even lacked the strength to call out to Odin. He waited for the terrible pain he knew would come when the shark made its first attack. And if there were others with him—he could not imagine the suffering he would have to endure before Death would finally come to claim him.

The fin vanished. He sensed the sea-denizen under

him and tried to draw away his legs. A moment later, Rafe felt it push against him. He was too exhausted to do anything more than wonder why nothing more terrible hadn't happened. There was another push!

The black fin came out of the water, circled around him, and leaped into the air.

"A dolphin!" Rafe shouted against the howl of the wind. He had heard many stories about this strange man-loving beast from the other galley slaves.

The dolphin leaped into the air again and, swimming close to Rafe, it rolled on its side, offering him its fin.

Gratefully Rafe took hold of the offered fin. The beast had saved his life. . . .

XXIII

Soon Rafe was riding the dolphin as easily as he had previously ridden a horse, though now the animal was not in any way under his control. The island faded from view. There was nothing but sun glinting on the open sea in every direction. Daylight waned. When the moon came up, it silvered the top of the waters. Though the dolphin slowed its pace, it never stopped.

Rafe found himself drifting into a light slumber that was filled with strange dreams, one of which placed him back in time when he was a boy. . . .

He was standing beside Gumpa, on the bank of the river not far from the stronghold. A Viking ship lay smoldering a short distance upstream from where they were. Gumpa grasped several gold pieces in his left hand, and with his right hand he held up one of them. After studying it for a long time, he said, "I think one day you will do something like this." And he handed the piece of gold to Rafe.

The boy looked at it. Incised into it was the figure of a man astride an animal that looked like a large fish. "What kind of a horse is that?" Rafe asked.

"Not a horse . . . Not even a fish, but something men of the sea call a dolphin," Gumpa answered. "I have heard stories about it when I was in Miklagard. . . . The Vikings and other men of the sea say that of all of the creatures who live in the sea, the dolphin is the most like man and the friendliest to him." Then looking toward the Viking ship, he added, "Gold pieces like this one are even hard to come by in Miklagard. They come from another place to the west of that country."

Rafe returned the gold coin to Gumpa. . . .

The second dream that visited Rafe brought him back to the present and gave him the peculiar feeling that he was astride the naked body of the woman with olive skin, black flashing eyes, and long black hair. So intense was the sensation that he could not quell the passion that was beginning to flare in him. The woman was tempestuously yielding. His man-thing swelled and her undulations culled his fluid from him. He released it with a groan of pleasure so loud that it penetrated his light slumber and woke him to a reality that for someone else would have seemed a dream.

The dolphin swam into the dawn of a new day with pink clouds that were soon yellowed by the sun and then disappeared altogether, leaving an azure blue sky. The sea was very calm. In some places, Rafe could see far into its depths and he beheld sights more wondrous than he could have ever imagined.

There were great mountains, whose summits never broke the surface of the sea and whose bases were beyond the range of Rafe's sight. There were flat open plains and long spans of gently rolling hills. There were the wrecks of proud ships and the skeletons of the men who sailed them.

But the most remarkable thing he saw were the ruins that were huge places of stone, where many people had once dwelled. Buildings with stone columns and stone walkways were deep beneath the surface of the sea. Strongholds where men once dwelt were now occupied by a variety of splendidly colored fish. That they could have vanished beneath the sea was almost beyond his understanding. But he had experienced the sea's fury and he knew all too well that when the earth moved, so did the sea. Very often the sea came up and devoured the land, yet other times the bottom of the sea would break free to rise up above the water, giving new land to the people who survived.

Once they passed over a plain on which a great battle had been in progress when the sea took the land on which the men had fought. Everywhere there were the skeletons of the combatants. With them were their weapons and their shields. Both sides had perished. The right or wrong of one or the other's cause mattered less than the snap of a finger. Their force of arms was nothing when compared to the cataclysm that plunged them beneath the sea.

Rafe was so involved with his thoughts, he failed to realize that other dolphins were swimming close by and between them there was a great deal of chatter. One came very close, popped its head out of the water, and took a good look at him. Then, with what sounded like a laugh, it did a backward somersault into the sea.

Rafe laughed so hard he almost lost his hold on the dolphin he rode.

The day passed quickly. By the time the sun was low in the western sky, Rafe saw the sharp silhouette of some mountain peaks. With the coming of night, the mountains grew darker and more substantial.

The dolphin swam closer and closer to the land and when it was parallel to a sandy beach it rolled over on its back, dislodging Rafe from his place on it. And after leaping into the air several times, it headed out for the open sea, while Rafe turned and swam toward the beach.

A short time later, he was out of the water and walking along the sandy strip; he saw the light of a small fire a short distance in the woods that began just above the beach. He caught the scent of roasting meat, which made his mouth water and his stomach growl. Crouching, he approached the fire, ready to fight if need be for a piece of meat.

But there in the wavering reddish light of the fire, he saw Talum. She was busy roasting a rabbit.

"Talum," he whispered, too surprised to make his voice any louder. "Talum!"

"Eh, who is that?" she called out, standing.

Rafe," he answered, raising himself up and walking out to her. "Rafe."

She nodded. With a toothless grin, she waved him closer.

He ran and embraced her. "I thought you were killed by the earth heave," he said.

"You told me to become a crow and I did," she replied.

"And a dolphin too?" he asked, holding her at arm's length.

"That would take a great deal of magic," she laughed. "Much more than I possess."

He shook his head to show that he did not believe her. But he was too happy to see her to openly disagree, and he said, "I would have you here, no matter how you came." Again he drew her to him. But this time her scent was different; it was no longer sour and musty but rather sweet, something like new-mown hay.

"Come," she said, freeing herself, "eat and drink."

"You have mead?" he asked, squatting down by the fire.

"Wine," she answered. "Wine made from the grapes of summer." And she handed him a small cruse. "Drink as much as you want, as much as you want."

Rafe broke the clay seal and drank. The wine was

red, fruity, and subtly spiced. It filled him with a pleasant warmth. He nodded and said, "I am glad you have more wine."

"Much more," Talum assured him.

Rafe ate most of the rabbit and drank a substantial amount of wine, while he related his various adventures to Talum.

While he spoke, she did not interrupt or make a single gesture that would have stopped him. But when the pauses between his words became longer and longer, she told him, "You do not have much time, Rafe. . . . Even now Enlil is close by. He has come to do what no man could do and what he himself could not do in his many different forms. He will be himself when he confronts you."

Rafe nodded. Her voice came to him as if she were a long way off, not seated across the fire from him. He drank more wine and said, with a shake of his head, "I understand none of Enlil's anger against me, or the things you told me about the gods."

"You will understand everything," she assured him, "everything . . . But now you must come with me." She stood up and extended her cold bony hand to him. "Come," she urged. "Come."

"I am tired," Rafe answered. "My adventures have cost me my youth. . . . Look at me, Talum, look at me and tell me what you see."

"I see a man who has changed as the spring changes to the hoarfrost of winter. . . . I see a man who has seen much and has learned even more."

"I sought my destiny, Talum, and I have not found it; I have found only the prospect of yet another bloody battle with a demon named Enlil. . . . What have I to do with him or he with me that I have come to this place—wherever we are—to fight him?"

"Come," she said. "Come and as we go, I will try to answer your questions."

Rafe scrambled to his feet and took hold of her hand, which he found suprisingly warm and not in the least bit bony.

"I will tell you where we are," Talum said. "We are on an island in the southern sea, the place where Inanna lives. From here she governs the coming of spring and the passing of winter. It is here Enlil will come to claim her and in her womb plant the seed for a race of monsters that will feed upon the people of the earth. . . . Creatures like the Fomoiri, who were his progeny, but not clever enough to leave their mountain dwelling and go among men as men with the avowed purpose of devouring them."

From the quaver in her voice, Rafe knew she was frightened. But rather than draw attention to it and perhaps shame her, he kept silent.

"And as for what you are to him and he is to you," Talum continued, after clearing her throat, "you are the only obstacle standing in his way. . . . You must die if he is to achieve his goal."

"But why should I stand in his way?" Rafe questioned. "I only knew Enlil when he was Borit, the priest in Gumpa's stronghold, and though it is true that I fought him in his various forms, I only did it to survive."

"You will fight him again for the same reason," she said. "But this time, you will meet him as he is and if you survive so will all of mankind, and if you die so will all of mankind."

Rafe did not answer. The enormity of the disaster that would befall the race of man if Enlil were the victor was far more terrible than he might have imagined.

"Are you afraid?" Talum asked gently.

"Yes," Rafe answered. "I am afraid."

"Better to be afraid," Talum told him, "than foolish."

Together they moved through the woods to the center of the island, where the mountains drenched with moonlight rose straight up out of a flat open plain.

"Here you will fight him," Talum said, waving her hand so that its movement encompassed all of the length and breadth of the open area that lay before them. "But hurry, we do not have much time."

They moved across the plain with surprising speed. In a very short time they were at the base of the mountains. Huge boulders were everywhere.

Talum threaded her way between them until they came to a small, open area, where there was a circle of upright stones, similar to the one Rafe had seen on the river. He was about to ask Talum if she remembered the one on the river, when suddenly a gnomelike man came out of the shadows. In the moonlight the hump on his back was still clearly visible.

"He is here, Tyr," Talum said, speaking to the stranger.

The gnomelike man came closer. His skin was brown with age and as seamed as old dry leather. He looked at Rafe for a long time, moving his beady eyes up and down several times. With his eyes still on Rafe, he asked Talum, "Are you sure that what you will give will not be as terrible as what you seek to avoid?"

"I am not sure," she answered softly.

"Then why—"

"I am a woman," she said, "and because I am, the alternative is unthinkable."

"Sooner or later it will be turned against us," Tyr said.

Rafe moved his eyes from one to the other. Though he understood the words, he did not understand what they were talking about.

"The old must make way for the new," Talum said. "The gods change, though their changing takes much longer than most things. . . . The people change them, even if they do not want to be changed."

Tyr nodded and with a motion of his hand, he beckoned Rafe to follow him. "She cannot come," he told him. "It is only for men."

Rafe looked questioningly at Talum, but she nodded and turned away.

The gnome beckoned again and this time Rafe followed him. They went behind some huge boulders and into a cave. The embers of a low fire glowed red in a stone basin. Nearby was a stone anvil and several metal tongs.

"You will do everything I do," Tyr told him. "You will say everything I say."

"To what end?" Rafe questioned.

"To be the champion of mankind," the gnome answered with a lopsided grin. And before Rafe could answer, Tyr whirled around three times, crying out for the fire to help him draw the metal from the rocks.

Rafe imitated him.

The fire suddenly blazed up.

Tyr gathered several large red rocks and put them in the fire, calling out to them to be patient for their bride.

Rafe did exactly the same thing.

Tyr placed handfuls of charred wood into the flames and then prayed for the union of rock and wood to be fruitful. Then chanting about the strength of the child, he worked a bellows made of pigskin.

Rafe worked the bellows and sung Tyr's words.

The cave became very hot. Sweat poured from Rafe's body but he continued to pump the bellows.

Tyr put more red rocks into the flames and more charred wood. Then he took the bellows and told Rafe to do and say as he had.

213

When the whole cave glowed red with fire and the walls were hot to the touch, Tyr broke a clay seal at the bottom of the basin. Instantly a thin white stream of smoking liquid spurted out of the hole and poured into a narrow trench.

"The gods took kindly to the union," Tyr said with a characteristically lopsided smile.

Rafe was fascinated by the white-hot stream. He had often watched the smiths in the stronghold as they joined molten red copper and white tin to form the yellow bronze that they later hammered into swords, knives, spears, and arrowheads, even into the killing end of the battle-axes. But this was different; here the metal came from the union between the red rocks and the charred pieces of wood. It was the progeny of the two and truly a wonder!

The stream of white-hot metal dwindled to a trickle and then ceased altogether, while in the trench the white was already turning to red, making it seem that somehow it had trapped the flames of the fire.

The bright rubescence rapidly changed to a darker hue, almost to the brown of dried blood.

"It is ready to be worked," Tyr said, and going to the side of the cave, he washed his hands in a small bowl and chanted prayers to a strange god to guide him in his task.

Rafe imitated all of Tyr's acts and words.

Then Tyr went to the narrow trench, where the smoldering metal was now covered with a dark brownish-red crust. With a pair of metal tongs, he lifted the smoking strip onto the stone anvil. Taking a huge hammer in his right hand, he began to beat the metal. Sparks flew in every direction and the blows of the hammer filled the narrow confines of the cave. "Blow air into the fire," the gnome shouted above the din.

Rafe worked the bellows until the fire made the stone bowl that held it glow red.

Tyr took the strip of metal he was hammering to the fire and plunged it into the flames. "Watch carefully," he admonished Rafe, "so that you will be able to show others if you survive." The gnome removed the glowing strip from the fire and brought it back to the anvil. "Now you hammer it," he said.

Rafe picked up the hammer in his right hand. Holding the metal with the tongs, he worked the glowing substance across the anvil. Every part of it felt the blows of the hammer.

Once he looked up and saw his shadow on the wall of the cave. It was much, much larger than he was. Another time, he glanced at the gnome, who was busy pouring water into an old barrel.

"Now bring the metal back to the fire," Tyr shouted. Rafe obeyed him.

"Take it to the anvil, bend it back on itself, and continue to hammer it," Tyr said.

"Over and over Rafe repeated the same actions. His right arm ached from swinging the hammer and his body was covered with sweat.

"Give it to me," Tyr told him, "and I will shape it." With incredible swiftness the gnome cunningly worked the long strip into the form of a sword. Several times he bent the blade's edge back on itself and amid a shower of sparks hammered it into shape again. "You must do this to make the cutting edge and the point the strongest parts of the blade."

Rafe worked the edge of the blade and its point just as the gnome had.

"This is the most important part of making a good sword," Tyr said. Taking the glowing blade from Rafe, he plunged it into the barrel of water. With a loud hiss, a column of steam leaped up from the water. Again he held the blade in the fire and again he plunged it into the water. "The blade must cool now and then you will hone and fit a hilt to it," he said, pushing the blade deep into the earth of the cave.

"How long must we wait for it to cool?" Rafe questioned.

"Until night has fallen," Tyr said, going to the entrance of the cave and looking up at the sky. "Not long . . . not long at all." He stepped back into the half-light of the cave. "You must remember all you have seen here," he said, turning to Rafe.

"I will," Rafe replied.

"And if someone should be asked who taught you the secret of iron," the gnome said, "tell him that Tyr did."

"Yes, I will tell them that."

Tyr nodded, and taking a pipe from his pouch, he filled it with tobacco and lit it. He settled down against the back wall of the cave and contentedly smoked.

Rafe sat down near him. And for a while neither one of them spoke. But then Tyr asked, "Have you been with Inanna long?"

"I have never seen Inanna," Rafe answered.

"Then you have never looked," Tyr said with a lopsided smile, "or you are blind. I understand that it is a common malady among your kind."

With a shrug, Rafe replied, "Believe what you want, but I have never seen Inanna, except perhaps in dreams."

"I am always amazed," Tyr said with a laugh, "how the gods always manage to choose those from the race of man who in some way or other serve their purpose. . . . They impute to man the kind of wisdom that only they possess." He shook his head, closed his eyes and puffed on the pipe.

Rafe stood up and walked to the entrance of the cave. Though night had not yet arrived, the shadows were beginning to creep slowly over the lower portion of the mountains and weave themselves with dark gray light between the large boulders.

"Have you ever seen Enlil?" Rafe called to the gnome from the mouth of the cave.

Tyr did not answer.

Rafe repeated the question and, at the same time, he went back into the cave.

The fire was low but there was enough light for Rafe to see that Tyr was no longer resting against the back wall of the cave. Where the gnome had been were two stones: one for achieving a rough edge on the sword and the other for bringing it to a fine finish.

Rafe waited until darkness fell across the mouth of the cave before he removed the sword from the earth. He started to put an edge on the blade. He worked diligently. Before half of the night was gone, the blade shone like silver and its edge was fine enough to slice through a single hair of his beard.

Satisfied that he could not improve its sharpness, Rafe set about the task of fixing a hilt to it. Tyr had provided him with the ivory tusks of a boar and several pieces of metal already shaped into clamps. After a short while, the hilt was fitted to the blunt edge of the blade. The weapon was now complete and Rafe went to the rear of the cave to sleep.

He awoke at first gray light of the new day and with the sword in his hand, he hurried to where he had left Talum the previous day. He moved from boulder to boulder, remembering that it did not take him and Tyr long to reach the cave. The way he was returning was longer than it should have been. The boulders that should have been familiar were not.

Rafe stopped and looked around him. He had the strange sensation that many pairs of eyes were on him, yet he saw neither beast nor man. Once more he started to look for Talum but could not find her. Then suddenly he heard his name being called. Sure that Talum was calling him, he answered. "I am lost," he shouted. "I do not know where you are."

"I am here!" came the thunderous reply.

Suddenly Rafe saw Enlil. He was standing in front of him. Rafe's first impulse was to cower back against the rock and seek a way to flee before it was too late, before the hideous monster destroyed him.

Enlil loomed over him, like some great black cloud. His lips were red with dripping blood; his gaping jaws revealed the teeth of a wolf. He was part man and part demon. Armed with a great bronze sword and shield, he roared out his hatred for Rafe and for all of mankind. As Enlil bellowed, he became larger and larger, until the sun was obscured by him and the day turned into night.

In the unnatural blackness, Rafe saw Death's even darker form. He stood off to one side waiting to take one or the other of them, or perhaps both, if each should happen to strike a killing blow.

Rafe turned his eyes back to Enlil. The demon was more frightening to look at than Death himself. To look at Enlil was to see in one hateful creature all the hideous agony that could be afflicted on man. It was there in his blazing eyes; it was in his purpose.

Enlil screamed at Rafe and, swinging his great sword down, he tried to cleave him in two.

But Rafe heard the rush of wind. Knowing what the sound meant, he dropped to the ground and rolled away just as Enlil's sword came hurtling down. In an instant, he was on his feet and running to the largest open space he saw.

Enlil came racing after him.

Rafe suddenly found himself on the open plain in front of the mountains. There he saw Talum. He called to her.

"You must fight Enlil," she shouted at him. "You must turn and face him."

"I am too small and he is too large," Rafe called back.

Talum pointed her finger at him. "You will be whatever size he is," she told him.

In an instant Rafe was as large as Enlil. He turned and confronted the demon. The battle began in earnest as each one thrust and slashed at the other. Their movement back and forth across the plain raised huge clouds of dust and when one or the other of them stumbled, the earth trembled under him.

Enlil brought his sword down and sliced deeply into Rafe's left shoulder, making him stagger.

Death moved closer to Rafe and Talum gasped with horror.

Bleeding and exhausted, Rafe tried to thrust his sword into Enlil, but the demon's shield was always there to protect him.

The battle between them grew fiercer.

Enlil raised his sword for the killing stroke and brought it down with a mighty force that would have split apart any of the great boulders, had it struck one, but it crashed against Rafe's sword and broke apart.

Holding half of the quivering weapon in his hand, Enlil was too stunned to move.

The next instant, Rafe's blade slipped past the shield and went straight into the demon's heart.

Enlil clutched at his breast, trying to pull the blade out.

But Rafe pushed it deeper and deeper into the creature's chest. Black blood gushed from the wound.

Enlil dropped to his knees. He vomited blood.

As soon as Rafe pulled the blade free, he and the demon were once again the size of men.

Enlil toppled over and writhing in the dust he tried to escape Death's touch. But Death only laughed at his efforts. When the demon gasped his last breath, Death took hold of Enlil's spirit and forced it to follow him.

Rafe ran his arm across his brow, wiping the sweat from it. His sword was stained with the demon's black blood. Weak from the wound in his left shoulder, Rafe placed the point of his sword into the earth and supported himself on it as he watched Enlil's body decay and shrivel into bits of dust that were soon lifted by a sudden gust of wind that scattered them everywhere.

He nodded with satisfaction. He had come a long way and had experienced many hardships to finally reach this place. Now that he had vanquished Enlil he would continue to search for his destiny. He was certain that all of the things that had happened to him had fulfilled some purpose, something beyond his ability to comprehend.

He glanced up at the sky. The sun was no longer hidden and small puffs of white clouds dotted the blue expanse like the sails of so many ships.

He smiled and turned to where Talum should have been standing. She was not there. In her stead was the young woman with olive skin, long black hair, and black eyes. She wore a white gown and held out her hands to him. She was the woman he had seen so many times in his dreams.

"It has been such a long wait," she said, as he came toward her.

Rafe stopped. The wound in his shoulder pained him. His left arm was red with blood. He began to move again but his steps faltered. The earth, sky, and the woman began to spin. He shook his head. His vision cleared. The pain in his shoulder was gone. No longer was there blood on his arm. The wound had vanished.

"Come, Rafe," she called in a mellifluous voice, holding out her hand to him.

"Inanna?" he asked hesitantly, after wetting his lips. "Inanna?"

"Yes, Inanna," she answered, taking hold of his hand.

"Then you were—"

"Yes, I was Talum. . . . But from now on, I will always be Inanna."

Rafe drew her close to him. He put his lips to hers and pressed her body against his own.

"Soon," she whispered, "soon I will be yours." And separating herself from him, she took hold of his right hand. "Come," she said. "Come with me."

Rafe followed her, doing her bidding as he had done from the time he came upon Talum in the snowstorm, so long ago.

With incredible swiftness, Inanna led him to a grotto deep in the mountains. There she opened her naked thighs for him, making him forget all the other women he had ever known, and receiving from him pleasure so intense that, while it held her in its ineffable grip, her body quivered with an ecstasy that enchanced her feelings of womanliness manyfold. . . . Here, where god and man melted into one.

No spirit was wilder,
No passion greater
In vengeance or
in love

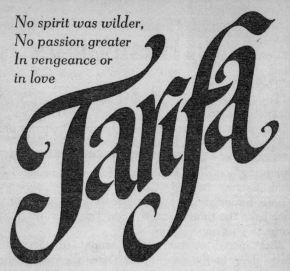

Tarifa

by Elizabeth Tebbets Taylor

She was a beguiling child, a bewitching temptress.
Many men worshipped her, many loved her,
some even tried to tame her. But only one man
could possess her. Bart Kinkaid, a daring sea
captain saw past her dark desires to the burning
within. Like ships in a tempest-tossed sea, their
love soared beyond the boundaries of time itself.

A Dell Book $2.5o

Dell Bestsellers

At your local bookstore or use this handy coupon for ordering: